First Printing, 2015

ISBN 978-0-9967738-0-5

http://www.secondwizardwar.com/

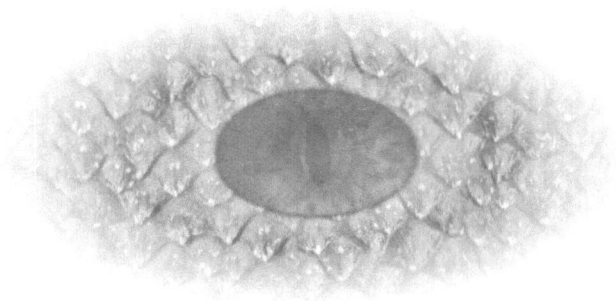

SECOND WIZARD WAR

VOLUME 1

CHAPTER 1

Arisa slept peacefully. It was rare that she got to sleep next to a warm fire at night. It took such effort to clear enough space for both her and the fire to burn safely that she seldom took the time. Especially when it had to be such a large fire to keep her warm. She had tried a smaller fire once and curled herself around it, but that had left her with a slightly singed tail.

"...et up!"

Arisa enjoyed the warmth, but wished she had made the fire just a little smaller. It was nice, but it was uncomfortable against her side now.

Crack

The heat felt like it was all around her. It was odd since camping fires never bothered her before, but right now it was beginning to feel very uncomfortable.

"...ake up!!"

Small hands. She had the distinct feeling of small hands pushing on her face. Who was it that had such a lack of etiquette to bother her while she was sleeping? She was finally having such a nice rest.

"Please, you have to wake up. If you don't..."

Arisa heard the small voice trail off into sniffles.

Crying? Why would someone be crying just

because I am sleeping?

The crackling she heard started to grow louder as she roused herself from what had been a very comfortable sleep. Whomever this voice belonged to had picked the wrong dragon to wake from sleep. Arisa did not anger easily but she was certainly annoyed that this voice would not leave her alone. Allowing one eye to open just a bit she mumbled at the target of her annoyance.

"Please leave me be, I am… Oh!"

Both of Arisa's eyes opened wide at the unexpected sight. All around her was a building engulfed in flames. When she opened her eye to address the voice she did not expect to see this. In fact she did not expect the voice and small hands to belong to a human child either. The child was crying and on its knees, practically lying against Arisa's face as it pushed against her scaled cheek.

"What is going on here? Where am I?"

Sob

Arisa's question went unanswered as the child continued to cry. Lifting her head away from the small human she took a quick look around at her surroundings. Looking back down Arisa nudged at the child to try and get a response yielded no results as it just kept crying into it's own hands. She didn't want to frighten it any more than it was but she needed to get its attention.

"Child!"

The body next to her flinched but finally looked up. Large bits of burning wood were now falling from above, some of them leaving red marks on the child.

"I don... I can't.. I can't find my mother!"

CRACK

Arisa jerked her head up and saw the burning roof sag and drop about a foot. It wouldn't last much longer before giving way completely.

Taking a better look around herself Arisa could see that the building, or at least what was left of a building, was on the verge of collapsing. One wall was completely missing, the remnants of it underneath her body. Outside the missing wall she could see other buildings, all engulfed in flames and falling in on themselves. The dark backdrop of the sky told her it was very late into the evening.

The small child was still looking up at her, tears streaming down her face as it continued to cry. If the heat was bothering Arisa, a dragon, then this child must be in severe pain from that same heat. Indeed, now that she looked more closely, Arisa could see that the child's entire skin was turning red even as it sat there staring at her.

"Come with me, we need to leave here."

Arisa slowly rose to her feet, being careful to not bring what remained of the building down around them. It wouldn't do more than cause her some pain and trouble, but it would very likely kill the small human next to her.

"Mom!"

The child didn't move. It remained on its knees crying, staring at the ground where Arisa had just been.

"You have to leave before the building collapses!"

"B-but mom. I can't find my mother!"

Another brief look around her told Arisa that there was little chance *mom* would be found, at least not alive. Most of the buildings that she could see through the missing wall had already collapsed in on themselves. Others were so engulfed in flames that it was difficult to imagine that anybody could be left alive. It was a miracle this child was still alive.

Another loud crack and a small rain of burning debris told Arisa it was past time to get out of here. She stepped over the child and moved out of the building. Once out of the structure she could finally raise her head up and look around her. She was in a small village, what was left of it. Everything burned.

Kawoosh

The building just down the street collapsed, sending a brilliant shower of sparks into the night sky. Arisa turned her attention back to the child who was still crying inside the burning building.

For heaven's sake...

Arisa stuck her head back into the building and carefully snatched the child up in her jaws.

"Nooo! I have to find mom and dad!"

"Ee have oo essape eefore we gurn ourhelfes".

Arisa could only mumble around the human that was dangling from her mouth.

Stretching her wings out to fly away from this burning nightmare caused her to wince in pain. Her right wing was badly singed. She had been laying on that side after, apparently, crashing through the burning wall in the building. She steadied herself and gave a small flap of her wings but once again winced at the pain that shot through her wing.

"Owww!"

"Sowwy."

Arisa had tightened her grip on the child from the pain.

She would have to find her way out of this labyrinth on foot. Trying to maneuver on the ground had never been easy for her. She was used to seeing things from the sky, using the sun, moon or mountains for reference while navigating. Tonight she had none of those.

The brilliance of the fire dimmed her vision, preventing her from seeing much past the flames, let alone to the nearest mountain. The sky above was filled with nothing but smoke so there was no moon to be seen either. Arisa swung her had back and forth looking for the quickest way out of this human-made maze, making the poor child in her mouth dizzy.

I guess it doesn't matter which direction I pick at this point.

Arisa turned to her left and began to quickly walk down the street, trying not to jostle the child too much as she avoided burning buildings. Thankfully this was more of a village than a city so the streets were wide enough for her to easily pass between the buildings. However, she still had to navigate around some of the burned walls that had crumbled out into the street.

"Mom! Dad!"

The child continued to wail for its mother. Arisa felt a small pang of regret for this small human. She knew in her heart that there was little chance of the child seeing its mother again. Her brief survey of the town told Arisa that it was unlikely that anybody else was alive. Any who had survived would be outside the town by now.

Water!

The smell arrived before the sound. Arisa could detect the scent of fresh water coming from somewhere ahead. She pushed on, trying to quicken her pace without causing her cargo too much discomfort. Shortly after came the trickling sound of a stream. That was a good sound. It meant they were likely near the edge of the village.

"Go back! My mom."

The child whimpered while Arisa continued past the buildings. Apparently, it sensed that they were about to leave the village as well.

Darkness ahead signaled the edge of the village and escape from the fire. Arisa breathed a sigh of relief. Once out of the village she would surely be able to find another human and deposit this little one with them.

A huge splash of water enveloped them as Arisa crashed into the stream. A dozen more steps saw her to a safe spot to deposit the child onto some grass.

Licking at the unpleasant taste in her mouth Arisa took the few steps back to the stream in an effort to wash away the taste of the soot and human. Now that their immediate safety was assured she wished to clean herself up a bit to inspect how badly burned her wing was.

Standing in the middle of the shallow stream Arisa took mouthfuls of water into her mouth and splashed it back. There was so much soot covering her she could not see her own scales

If this stream were deeper I could have just rolled in it to clean myself rather than have need to stoop to throwing water on m—ach!

Arisa winced in pain as the water cascaded down over her burnt wing. She steadied herself and dumped one more mouthful just at the top of her wing to let it fall down her side once more before turning her neck to inspect the wound.

"It will be days before I can even think about flying with my wing in this shape."

After complaining to no one in particular, Arisa turned and took the few steps back to the child. Her wing would likely heal on its own in time. However, she did not wish to even imagine the pain she would cause herself if she tried a sustained flight. The intensity of the pain from just a gentle flap earlier was something she could do without feeling ever again.

"There is nothing for it, I will just have to

walk like all the other beasts until it heals. Now to find some other humans and deliver this child to—."

She stopped in her tracks as she suddenly became aware of the silence. Being so absorbed in their escape and then checking her wing, Arisa had not noticed it before now. Of course she could hear the sound of the village still burning, of wood collapsing and exploding. She could hear the murmur of the stream as it trickled by. Even the quiet whimper of the child a few paces away could be heard. But — nothing else.

No cries of humans mourning the loss of their loved ones. No names being shouted across the fields as they searched for one another. Nothing. She could hear not a single human other than the one on the ground next to her.

This village was small to be sure, but someone should have survived. Surely not everyone could have slept through the entire village burning down around them except this one small child. Even if the fire started at one edge of the village and swept across to the other, someone should have managed to escape before death claimed them.

Arisa's eyes opened wide as she suddenly became worried with the realization that there was no one to leave the small human with.

Looking over at the child, Arisa confirmed what she already suspected from having carried it out of the village. It was too small. Small always meant young and this child would be too young to take care of itself. Arisa knew humans were not born with the ability to hunt and provide for themselves like dragons and other beasts. No, they had to be taught and learn for themselves. They had to be provided for until they learned.

Arisa was also worried for selfish reasons. She couldn't fly with her wing like it was. It might be weeks before she could fly again. Hunting from the ground was hard for dragons. No it was better to say it was nearly impossible. Dragons could not simply hide in the grass as they stalked their prey. They were meant to swoop down from the sky and take their meals from above.

She would normally seek an exchange with the surviving villagers. Arisa would ask them to provide food for her while she healed and in return she would provide labor to help them rebuild their village more quickly. Dragons could fell trees swifter than any human, even with the large teeth-like sticks humans often used to cut them down. She would also have been able to share a shelter with the villagers until a few houses had been rebuilt.

Another worry clouded her mind. Why had she herself had been in the village? She had no memory of coming here. The last thing Arisa could remember was flying.

What could have happened that she would end up inside a burning building? She could understand if the building had caught fire after she was already there. But her wing, which she had been asleep on, was burned by the fallen wall. That to her was enough proof that the village had been burning before she got there. Had she flown into the wall? What would possibly have happened to cause her to crash into a burning wall?

Arisa shook her head and tried to push those thoughts out of her mind. The issue was what to do right now. She looked at the now silent human sitting on the ground. The child was unmoving and had its face buried between its knees. After briefly pondering what she should do Arisa softly spoke to the unmoving human.

"You, what is your name?"

Arisa had called quietly to the child so as not to startle it. Even still her voice had been loud enough to be clearly heard yet the child didn't respond. Not even a twitch. Arisa gently nudged the child's shoulder with her muzzle. It hadn't been much but the child didn't resist the pressure and slowly fell onto her side. Arisa could see the eyes staring blankly ahead, still cloudy with tears.

Looking more closely she could see a slight rise and fall of the chest. A good sign, the child was still breathing.

It is still alive.

"Can you here me?"

"…"

After a moment of silence the child turned it's head slightly to look at Arisa. That was an improvement.

"Stay here and don't move."

Arisa softly commanded of the small child. She wanted to determine for certain if anybody else still lived.

Arisa craned her neck up as high as she could

and looked towards the part of the village that could be seen. They were not that far. If she could fly she would be able to traverse the entire village in just a few moments. As it was, she would have to run around the perimeter of the village and see if anyone had escaped.

She needed to know. Before she could make any other decisions, she needed to know what her options were. She took one last look back at the still huddled child. Still no movement, but it was breathing.

* * * * *

Arisa had travelled nearly three-quarters of the way around the village and not seen a single person. She had been nearly convinced, before even she began, that all had perished. But she had to be sure. But how? How is it a small child could have survived and all the grown people died?

She had found nothing. Not even any bodies of those who had died trying to escape. No dropped clothing. No smell of fresh blood or burned flesh. Absolutely nothing. No signs at all that people had even tried to escape. It was as if every person perished inside their own houses.

Could they still be inside the village? No. Nothing was left standing. She had not seen a single building that was not collapsed in on itself while she travelled around the outside of the village. Arisa was a dragon and was used to seeing death. It was required that she kill for her own food so death was not a new thing to her. She had expected to see bodies in the streets if nothing else.

She had found nothing.

Arisa stopped at what was apparently a pasture for farm animals, or it had been. The grass was completely burnt away. She could make out the form of a few partially burnt cows. It was the only sign she had found that anything ever lived in this village. And it troubled her greatly.

As she worried about what to do she resumed her journey around and back to the child. This time at a slow walking pace. Having confirmed that there were no other humans who had already escaped the fire or were still trying to, Arisa turned her thoughts to the child and what to do with it.

The cows had been a welcome sight and smell. It meant she had some food for the next day or two. Maybe three if she was lucky. After that she could go some time without eating. She wouldn't care for the charred meat, though she believed she would find some raw meat if she dug into the cows a bit.

The child was another matter.

Arisa would manage eating the questionable meat. Humans were much more frail. It was very likely the child would become sick if it tried to eat the cow meat as well.

Upon returning to where she had left the child, Arisa could see that it had moved somewhat. Well, one could hardly call it movement exactly. It was more of a relaxed posture in the same position.

The child clung less tightly to itself and had stretched its legs out slightly. But even that little bit made Arisa feel better as she addressed the child.

"Can you talk now? You should have been able to rest long enough to be communicative by now."

It responded to the sound of her voice and looked up.

"Well! What is your name child? Or do you expect me to just keep calling you *you*?"

Hic

The child gulped and recoiled slightly at Arisa's tone. That response did not go unnoticed by Arisa. She tried to soften her voice and lowered her head in an attempt to put the child at ease.

"It is alright, I did not intend to startle you. Can you not tell me your name?"

"..."

Arisa sighed. "I suppose I can continue to call you *you*. But I must say that is not a very polite way to refer to someone. It is also a little vague as someone would never know if I am referring to you or another. But if that is what I must do then I will simply have to put up with having people give me strange looks when I call you *you*. Perhaps they will just think you are a pet of mine. Would you like to be my pet? I cannot imagine you find that to be very much fun."

Arisa had been told she talked a lot. In fact she enjoyed talking when anybody would listen. Though nobody else ever seemed to enjoy how much she talked. Generally she would try and refrain from talking so much. In this case, however, it gave her the opportunity to try and draw a few words out of the silent child.

"—ànde."

"What did you say?"

"My n—name. It's Elànde."

The child was barely whispering. Arisa could easily make it out as she had good ears, even for a dragon. But there was no reason to let the child know that. It would be good for the child to learn to speak more clearly.

"I'm sorry, could you speak up? I cannot quite hear you. This stream is so very noisy. All I hear is *woosh* and *gurgle*. Sometimes I think the stream also says *clunk* but I think it better to believe that is what the rocks in the stream are saying. Have you ever spoken with rocks before?"

The girl made a small noise that with more effort might have been called a giggle. It was not much but it did put Arisa's mind at ease, just a little bit. The child spoke up again, this time putting a little more effort and volume behind the words.

"No, I haven't."

"Well, I have. Though I suppose it would be more accurate to say that I have spoken *to* rocks. I am afraid to say they are not very communicative. But they are wonderful at listening. So, once again, could you say your name loud enough that I can hear you over this confounded stream?"

"It's Elànde. Elànde Kutàre."

"I see. Elànde. But isn't that a…"

Arisa stared at the small human before her. The name sounded female, but it looked like it was male. The nearby flames had begun to die down so the light was not as good to see details by. It's face certainly looked male. It had none of the prominent features found in human females. Skin is rough, chest is flat, hair is —

Oh!

There. On the left side of her head. A single clump of hair that reached down below the shoulder. As Arisa looked more closely it seemed the short hair might be due to the fire. It was very uneven and looked singed on the ends.

"So, you are a female then?"

Human children were so difficult to tell apart for her. Especially at young ages it was truly a struggle to tell the males from the females. It wasn't as if Arisa had never met a human female before. But there was something about this child that bothered her. Something that bothered her even more knowing it was a female.

"Huh?"

"You. Are you a female? You know what a female is don't you? My goodness. Even if we are out in the middle of nowhere one would think they would have taught you what a female is."

"A girl?"

"Correct. Very good. A girl is a female. I see you have had some schooling. So are you a female?"

"Y-yes. Of course I'm a girl."

"I see."

…

Arisa had been staring at her, wondering what to do with this child. A human female was even more trouble for her. Females were even more helpless at a young age. And there was still something that nagged at her. Everything about this situation Arisa had awoken to disturbed her.

Here she was, in the middle of nowhere at a village that was in the midst of being burnt to the ground. She had no memory of how she got there and was herself likely saved by the single survivor of the village taking time to wake her up. The fact that Arisa had slept as long as she did inside a burning structure made it obvious enough that she would have not awoken by herself. And this lone survivor was a child, a young girl. Not only was this girl the only survivor but there had been no signs of any other humans even attempting to flee.

"Umm, w-what is y—your name?"

"Oh. I am Arisa daughter of Tirza. I suppose I should have introduced myself. I am terribly sorry. I suppose with all the running and splashing I have forgotten my manners. I must really be more careful about such things. It is a disservice to all dragons for me to forget something so obvious and important as proper etiquette."

Elànde, now sitting upright, nodded slowly while shifting to look at the village. Following the child's gaze Arisa also looked upon what was left of the village.

"You woke up."

Arisa was surprised by the statement and saw that the girl was looking back at her again.

"I what?"

Obviously the girl was expecting a more intelligent answer.

"Oh. Yes, I guess I was asleep earlier. Though I do not know if you could properly call it being asleep. I believe I may have crashed into that building and been knocked unconscious."

She felt like an idiot at being surprised by this child. She also felt rather foolish for having to admit that she might have fallen out of the sky. Arisa prided herself in being calm and thinking things through rationally. She would feel much better after a proper night's sleep and a chance to think through everything that had happened this past hour.

"Do you know where my mother is? I... couldn't find her. She wasn't at home."

The girl no longer had tears in her eyes. There probably wasn't a single drop left that she could shed. Arisa watched as Elànde drew her knees up and wrapped her arms around them. The slight trembling could have been from the cool air, but it was more likely due to a different reason.

"How old are you Elànde?"

"I turned ten during the last moon."

"Ten hmm? Well that is a very good age. No, I am sorry I do not know where your mother is. I looked but I could not find anybody."

"Oh."

Elànde swayed slightly where she sat. Arisa feared this girl would again topple over at any moment if she did not lay down first.

"You should sleep now. It is dark and there is nothing we can do just now. We will look again when it is light out. Until then you should rest. I will need you awake and ready tomorrow so we can figure out what to do, alright?"

"Okay."

Arisa held no real hope at finding anybody alive in the village in the daylight. Even though the fire and dancing shadows made it difficult for her to see, her hearing was quite excellent. She would have heard anybody cry for help. As much as she hated to think of it this way she would have smelled the burnt flesh of any remaining humans as well. Arisa cringed inwardly at how to deal with Elànde once she was awake enough to ask even more difficult questions, like if her mother was dead.

For now, Arisa would sleep and hope her dreams would bring her some answers. Anything to help her understand what happened to the village, and to herself. Especially something that would explain how she came to be inside that burning building.

The girl hadn't moved. She continued to sit up, staring at the now smoldering village. Arisa moved around the child and laid down with her head near the girl. Wrapping her tail around Elànde, Arisa drew her back and muttered quietly.

"Sleep."

No longer able to see the village the girl finally laid down on her side. She still had her knees drawn up but her arms had relaxed slightly and her head now rested against Arisa's cheek.

"There will be nothing to harm you while I am here," Arisa told her. "You can sleep without fear. The fire will not be able to reach you. The stream will prevent it from coming close and I will be sure to wake you if something happens."

Elànde nodded slightly as Arisa heard the child's breathing begin to slow.

What have I gotten myself into. I should have just left it in that building and taken care of only myself. Now I have to take care of a child too young to do anything but slow me down.

It would be difficult for Arisa to find food without being able to fly, but it would not be impossible. The trouble was how long it would take to gather food. She could go a couple days without eating before it became a concern for her. But humans... Humans needed to eat every day and they usually ate more than once each day. How they could eat so often Arisa could not fathom.

Either way, it was an problem. A fully grown human could have at least been of use to her. But what could a child do? It was just a mouth to feed. A mouth that had to be fed at least once a day, and for a child more often than that. And hunting from the ground would take a great deal of time with very little to show in return.

I can not remember how I got here. For that

matter I can not even remember where I am. If I could fly I am sure I could find another village within a few days walk for the child, but like this…

I should just leave it behi—no. Not it. She is a female, a girl. A male child would have enough trouble fending for itself. A girl would have even more trouble.

While all dragons learned to hunt and fend for themselves, Arisa knew that in human society that wasn't the case. Most human males were in charge of gathering food. Females were often left at home to mend clothes and prepare the food gathered by the males. Even if this young girl could manage to prepare any food, she would not be capable of gathering the food at her age.

Arisa sighed.

As much as she wished that she could just leave the child behind and take care of herself… It just was not possible. She had never been able to just ignore those in need if they asked for help.

Arisa looked at her damaged wing as she mused the possibilities available to her. Not that she could think of that many to begin with.

This girl hadn't asked for help, but she had probably saved Arisa's life by waking her. Dragons were resistant to fire, but that didn't mean they wouldn't eventually burn. The singed wing was enough evidence of that to Arisa. Knowing that, she could not just leave the child behind to die.

I suppose I… that is we, will have to manage somehow.

CHAPTER 2

Elànde awoke sore and confused. She couldn't figure out where she was. She was sitting up with her knees pressed against her chest. It was not a comfortable way to sleep and her muscles told her so in no uncertain terms.

In front of her was a purple... something. No, not purple. Violet. She wasn't sure what it was. Why wasn't she in her own bed comfortably asleep? She tried to sit up a bit taller to get her bearings and heard a voice above her.

"Oh ho, so you are awake little one."

"Wha!"

Elànde cried out as she scrambled over the violet log in front of her.

"Ouch! Be more careful where you step. I may have scales but that does not mean I do not feel pain when you stomp on my tail."

Elànde looked up to see where the voice was coming from.

It's... huge!

Wide eyed, she stared up at the dragon. It was the same dragon from last night. But in the daylight it was so much bigger!

"Do you remember where you are? Do you remember what happened last night?"

"I remember the fire."

"Do you remember my name, Elànde?"

She stared up at the dragon, trying to remember its name. It apparently expected her to know it's name so she must know it.

"Oh! Is—is it Arisa?"

"Yes child, that is my name. I am very happy you remember my name. One's name is very important so it is good to put all effort possible into remembering names."

Elànde smiled at the praise.

But it lasted only a moment.

Her face suddenly fell and tears began to well up in her eyes. The tears began to roll down her cheeks as the horror of last night came back to her in a rush.

She sobbed openly now at the memory of seeing the village burn down around her. The horrifying sound echoed in her mind and she fell to her knees.

The dragon remained silent while Elànde cried. She fell forward and wrapped her arms as far around the dragon's face as she could and continue to cry against the softer scales.

She remembered everything.

Fire.

Heat.

Falling buildings.

Last night. She had awoken to the sound of wood crackling and popping. The sight of flames outside her window trying to get inside. She had run to her parents room but they were not there. Every room, every closet was searched while the rest of the house began to burn around her and still she could not find them anywhere.

The sound of burning and small explosions continued to echo in her mind. The roof of her house had crackled and begun to smoke with fire. She had run to the door to get outside when there was a huge crash nearby.

It was because of the dragon in front of her. The dragon had crashed through a wall into the building across the road from her house. She could see the dragon lying in the building, not moving. With her own home on fire she had run out of the house. Elànde had only been half way across the street when she had been thrown to the ground by a fierce eruption of heat and fire behind her.

Looking back she saw her house. It was not just burning now. It was completely engulfed in flames. The roof had fallen into the house, destroying everything she had ever known. Frozen with fear she could do nothing but watch from the middle of the road.

Buildings continued to implode and collapse around her. She finally managed to get back to her feet and stumbled into the building through the missing wall. Before her was a dragon. The same dragon whose face she was crying on. The same dragon that had carried her out of the building and out of the village.

Elànde didn't remember it all, just a vague memory of being picked up and carried. Through her tears all she could remember seeing was a blur of fire all around her. It had been unbearably hot as they had passed burning building after building. Finally the sound of water. The cool splash of water against her as they crossed the village stream. She didn't remember much after that.

Her tears began to slow and she just sobbed quietly against her savior before finally looking up at the dragon.

"My parents."

Elànde spoke very softly.

"They died, didn't they?"

The dragon slowly pulled her head away and nodded.

"I cannot be sure, but I believe that to be what has happened."

Elànde looked around them and saw no one. No people she knew. Nobody from the village. Not a single living person could be seen.

"Am—I alone?"

Arisa thought for a moment before responding.

"I believe so. I looked last night for anyone but could not find a single person outside the village. I will go look again inside the village itself now that the fires are out. Maybe I will be able to find a few people still alive."

Elànde nodded but didn't say anything. She looked up at Arisa and saw the dragon looking past her towards the village. Without looking down the dragon began to speak once again.

"Do you know what happened last night? What happened in the village to cause everything to catch on fire?"

"I don't... I don't know. Everything was just b—burning. It wouldn't stop."

"Will you be alright if I leave you alone for a little bit? I do not know if anybody else is alive but I need to find out. If somebody were to be alive and we left them here in trouble it would be very unkind of us."

"I want to come with you. I can help look."

"Absolutely not. I do not know what we may find in the village. You may not like what there is to see."

"But—"

"No. You must stay here."

"Will you be long?"

"I will go as quickly as I may. The village is not large, but it may take some time to check everywhere. I would feel very bad if I did not ensure that every building had been checked. If anybody is there and hurt they would not live long by themselves."

Elànde nodded silently.

"I will make haste. If it begins to take too much time I will come back and check on you before finishing."

Arisa slowly stood and moved away from her and towards the village. Elànde watched her as she entered the village. She saw her look back once before beginning her trek through the wreckage.

"I want to... feel better. I want to, but I miss my mother."

* * * * *

Arisa looked back at the child and saw that she hadn't moved. She thought briefly of going back but decided against it. The child appeared calm right now and she really needed to check the village.

In truth, she didn't believe she would find anybody alive. She had searched carefully the night before, but it was possible people had been hiding. Some humans she had met would build caves underneath their houses to hide in. It was possible the humans of this village did the same. If so they might have survived the fire. She would have to search carefully in and around each building to try and find any buried entrances to the human caves.

Through most of her search Arisa was able to see Elànde still sitting where she had left her — such was the utter completeness of the destruction. Very few walls remained standing. Most of those were parts of the building near the fireplace. As such they were made of stone instead of wood. The search was not taking as much time as she had thought it might. Rubble smoldered everywhere that Arisa looked.

How the girl had survived this ruin could not be fathomed. For that matter Arisa herself would likely be dead if the child had not managed to wake her up.

Her muzzle was already covered in black

soot from nosing through the debris around the sides of the buildings, looking for any cellars. So far she had not found any even though she had checked more than half the village.

The remnants of a wall collapsed as she was checking around it for any cellar doors in the ground. It had been a stone wall, but the stones had cracked under the tremendous heat of the fire. Arisa had barely touched it and yet it still fell. It depressed her to think that so many people could have died in one night.

She was near the far edge of the village. On this side there were fewer buildings and they had been spaced farther apart. It appeared that over here is where the farmers lived. The abundant land around the structures looked as if it had been used to grow vegetables. Now it was just charred black. Arisa glanced back at Elànde and saw that she was now kneeling next to the stream, making some effort to clean herself up. Arisa went back to checking the last few piles of rubble for signs that anybody might have escaped the fire.

When she finished checking Arisa saw that the farmland near some of these houses hadn't been completely burned up. Because the vegetables were so short in the ground they did not provide much fuel for the fire. Finding a spot near the edge that looked fairly unscathed she was able to gently claw at the ground to see what grew there.

Carrots. I think they are carrots.

She dug through a little more ground and managed to pull out a half dozen of the orange vegetable.

Arisa gathered them up in her mouth. They were covered in dirt and that did little to please her. However, she decided it was better to have the child eat something before they did anything else. Once her small companion was able to move about she could lead Elànde here to help dig up and carry more of the carrots if needed.

Taking a moment to look at her surroundings the dragon saw a forest that spread from the east to the north of the village. To the south the ground spread out and rolled along in small hills. She could see nothing in that direction that might provide a meal anytime soon. In the west, past where she had left the human, the land turned rocky and mountainous. There was virtually no chance of going that way in her current flightless condition.

Arisa sighed and made her way back to the child, passing down what appeared to be the main path through the village. Having nothing more to occupy her thoughts she looked around sadly at the destruction. The thought that she had been unconscious while the village burned angered her.

Oh...

Suddenly a rather uncomfortable thought occurred to her. Up until now Arisa had not considered the possibility that she had something to do with the village's destruction. It was true she had no memory of last night, or possibly days before. Dragons had little need for keeping track of such things so the concept of the calendar eluded her. But she knew from her knowledge of the moon's cycles that she had lost either only a few days, or so many days that an entire cycle had passed.

The fact that she had no memory, the fact she was unconscious in a building she had crashed into, and the fact the village had been completely destroyed could not be unrelated. It was no coincident that those things happened at the same time, which meant it was possible. There could be a connection between herself and what happened here. She was a peaceful dragon. She had not gone mad like others of her kin occasionally did. But the possibility that she could somehow be involved with the burning of this village could not be denied.

Arisa pushed this thought to the back of her mind and continued her journey back to the child.

Even if I am somehow involved, what matters now is Elànde. I need to get her to another village that can care for her. Once that is done I can worry about myself and try to find a way to regain my own memories.

"Heer, yu ay eed diss."

Arisa mumbled through the carrots as she crossed the stream. After dropping them in a pile near the child she took a large drink from the stream to clear the taste of dirt from her mouth.

"Huh?"

The girl was looking at her, not having understood what the dragon said.

"I am sorry. It is difficult to talk when one's mouth is full. It is also a bad habit that you should not pick up. I would never normally do such a thing, but I suppose that these are not normal times for either one of us."

Elànde nodded silently.

"This is food that you may eat, though you may want to wash it off in the stream before doing so. I do not think you will find the taste any more appealing than I did until you have done so."

She examined her young companion. Arisa could now see that she looked much more a girl than she did last night. Having cleaned herself up she could see that the child had once had long hair. The soft hands probably meant she had not been sent out to the fields or any other places to do much work yet.

"I am going to leave you one more time. I found some cows that I will be able to eat but I do not think that you would want to watch. So you will need to stay here and eat your own food and I will return shortly."

"Wait! Did—"

Arisa knew the child must have questions about her attempts to find any survivors in the village. She understood the girl's hesitation. If Elànde asked her and she were to reply that she had found nobody alive it would destroy her last hope of seeing either of her parents again.

"I am sorry. I looked everywhere I could but I did not find anybody. It seems the two of us are the only ones to have left the village. But you do not need to worry yourself. I will make sure that you get to another village with humans that can care for you. For now you should eat."

"Mm."

It wasn't much of a response, but it was better than what Arisa expected. The child had probably spent the time alone thinking of nothing else than that she would never see her parents again. Being told as much was just the confirmation she had expected. Still... It was such a young child. Humans often relied on their elders for many years. Arisa wanted to do more for her but she knew not what. Getting her to another village was the best thing.

"I shall be back shortly. Eat what you can and then we will gather more before we leave. The water is cold but the sun is quite warm. It would do you good to try to wash your face and clean yourself up further. It may be the last chance you get for some time. I believe it would help you to feel better too."

"Alright."

* * * * *

Elànde watched the dragon move back off in the direction she had come from a moment ago. She sniffed back the tears that welled up in her eyes. Her mother was never happy to see her cry. She wouldn't be happy now either. She had to be strong so her parents wouldn't be sad now.

She picked up one of the dirty carrots and stared at it for a few moments slowly moving to the stream to wash it off. She didn't have the energy to do a very good job but managed to get most of the dirt off before taking a bite. She wasn't really hungry. Sore and tired, yes. Too tired to bring herself to do anything more than just nibble at the carrot.

After getting through little more than half the carrot she finally gave up and set it down before gathering the rest of the carrots. She took extra time washing each carrot, even past the time they were clean enough to eat. Elànde knew there was little point in washing the carrots this much, but she didn't want to continue sitting with nothing to do but think of her parents.

"Mother."

The loneliness terrified Elànde. She didn't know what she would do. Everybody she knew was in the village. If they had all… gone away, then she was by herself. She was alone. Her parents had told her of dragons. The villagers often talked about them. How they never stayed in one place too long. She knew Arisa wouldn't stay with her for more than a few days at best.

"Dragons are friendly to people, but they don't live like we do. They do not build houses to live in or even stay in one place. They fly around the world exploring and learning."

Her father had told her this once when she had asked him about them after hearing the villagers talking about dragons one day.

"They won't hurt us?"

"No sweet heart. There are very few dragons who would hurt anyone. The few that do try to hurt people are stopped by other dragons."

"You mean they attack their own kind to save us? Why would they do that?"

"Dragons enjoy knowledge and learning about things. Just like us, a dragon can only be in one place at a time. And just like us it takes them time to travel to a new place. If they had to learn everything themselves it would take forever. But if they come to a village like ours they can learn from all of us at once."

"So we teach dragons?"

"Yes, but they teach us too. When a dragon visits a village they tell us news from other villages. Sometimes from villages that would take us years to reach by foot."

Her father continued his tale. It was almost story-like to Elànde the way he told it. It had made her want to meet a dragon.

"And in exchange for the news they bring us we share what we have learned ourselves with them. We also give them some of our animals to eat. In thanks for food, they help us with our village by moving heavy things like trees and rocks for us."

"Ooohh... Will I get to meet a dragon someday?"

"I'm sure you will honey. One came a few years ago but you were too young to remember. The next time one comes I will make sure you get to meet them, okay?"

"Okay!"

She had been so excited at the time to see a dragon. Now she couldn't bring herself to be happy at all about it. All she could think of was that she would never again see her parents.

* * * * *

Arisa took an out of the way route back to her small companion. She wanted to stay downwind until she reached the stream so that she would have a chance to wash up a bit first. It would not be good for the child's trust level if she were to arrive smelling of fresh blood.

The meal had been good. A little well done for her taste. It had taken time to work through the carcasses and find the parts that had not been burned up along with the village. In the end it was more trouble than she would have liked but it was enough food to satisfy her for a couple days. Hopefully it would not take that long to find a home for this child and a place for her own wing to heal.

Splashing her face around in the stream she managed to wash all the blood away and most of the smell. Arisa doubted the child's nose would be able to detect what remained. She drank deeply from the cool water before heading back to her new friend.

Friend? Well I suppose one could call us acquaintances since we have met, although it has only been a short period of time. Certainly I would refer to us as companions for the moment at the very least. We are after all going to be traveling together for a short while. It would only be natural to call us traveling companions.

I cannot imagine being friends with a human though. She is nice I am sure but to be friends with a human? That would just not be possible. I will find a place for her to live and stay. Then after a few days rest I will leave and probably never see her again. In such a case I cannot possibly think to call her a friend. Dragons just do not stay in one place long enough to make friends like that.

As she was pondering this Arisa came to where Elànde still knelt by the stream. The pile of carrots next to her was clean. One carrot lay a few feet away, about three-quarters of it having been eaten. The pile of remaining carrots did not seem any smaller than what she had originally brought so it was doubtful the child had eaten more than that one carrot.

Elànde was just finishing washing her arms. Arisa could now see that, with the dirt and soot cleaned off, she wore a bracelet on her left wrist. The girl was stretching to reach around herself in an awkward attempt to clean her back. Her face was wet, showing the signs that it too had been washed. Even though Arisa already knew she was a girl, the much cleaner face now made it obvious this was a girl.

"You look much more like a lady when you are clean, child."

"Oh!"

The child startled a bit, apparently not realizing Arisa was now standing only ten feet away from her.

How a person can not notice a full-size dragon approach is a wonder. I shall have to remember this, it will be a good story to tell someday.

Arisa snorted at the thought of being able to sneak up on this child.

"T-thank you. The water is so cold it is hard to wash."

"I see."

Arisa gave a slow nod.

"Then I shall let you finish bathing. When you are done we shall decide what to do and where to go. We must find another nearby village. You cannot possibly live off carrots for the rest of your life and I do not believe I am best equipped to provide food for a human child."

Elànde nodded and turned back to the stream and worked to finish washing her back. After a short time she was evidently content with the effort. Having no way to dry herself she simply let her shirt fall back down over her back. It looked to Arisa that it stuck to the child's skin in a rather uncomfortable manner. The sun was already quite warm so she would dry rather quickly.

"I am finished."

Arisa looked the child over carefully. Yes, she indeed had once had longer hair. Now that it was somewhat clean it was obviously meant to be an auburn. Or more specifically, it was closer to being chestnut colored. Her hazel eyes matched well to her hair color. She was certainly cleaner, but had a long way to go before one could properly call her clean.

"What was your mother's name?"

The girl froze for a moment at the mention of her mother before responding.

"It… was Marlene."

"So you are Elànde daughter of Marlene

then."

The child simply stared back, looking somewhat confused.

"It is how dragon's refer to each other. We do not have family names. Instead we are named after our parents in such a way."

"Oh, I see."

"Good! Then let us decide what we shall do now. Do you know of any nearby villages?"

"Umm, Yes. But…"

Arisa waited for the child to continue.

"…"

"Unless you finish your statement I will not know what you mean. We dragons have many powers but reading minds is not one of them."

"I don't know the way."

"That is not entirely unexpected. Why were you hesitant to say so? Did you think I would be angry with you?"

Elànde nodded.

"Why would you think I should be angry with you?"

The young girl looked down and mumbled something too soft even for the dragon's ears to pick up.

"I am sorry I could not hear you?"

"You're scary… a little."

Arisa was taken aback at hearing that. It was true she was much larger than the child. But she did not think she had been particularly scary.

"Oh. Well. Again I am sorry. I do not wish to seem scary. I really am not, I promise. And I am certainly not angry with you. You are a *child* and I would not expect you to know exactly how to get there. That is something for adults to know."

The girl flinched at the word *child*. Sighing softly, Arisa quietly chastised herself for unintentionally sounding as if she thought *children* knew nothing.

"Do you know how far the village is? People from your own village must go trading with the people from that village. How long does it take them to travel there and back?"

"My father went one time. He said he would be gone for seven nights."

Arisa mused over this information. A seven day trip. That probably meant six days of travel and one day at the neighboring village to conduct trade business with them.

Three days. Three days at the speed the villagers would normally travel. If they were going to trade then it is very likely that they would have used a horse drawn cart to carry their wares. I could get there well before the moon rises if I could fly, but walking at the speed of this child...

She looked at the child watching her.

Too far. She would tire easily. That journey would easily take a grown man four days or more by foot. For this child I would expect no less than five days, probably six. And that is not taking into account the time needed to find food for her to eat. If that is even possible.

There was a solution. Arisa knew this but she hated the idea. Dragons were noble creatures. The thought of stooping that low, even to save this child, was difficult for her to accept. To Arisa's way of thinking it was, simply put, beneath her.

But there was no other option she could think of. It was the only viable choice open to her. She addressed the child before her, steeling her resolve to see to this small child's safety.

"It will take too long for you to walk there. You are small and would need to travel much slower than the adults from your village. I do not believe we would make it before something were to happen to you. It is possible for me to travel much more quickly, even on the ground. Therefore..."

But it is just so unbecoming.

"... you will need to ride on my back. That will let us travel much faster and farther each day."

Arisa saw the child's eyes grow far rounder than she would have thought was possible.

CHAPTER 3

Elànde hurt in places she didn't think was possible. She had ridden with her father on his horse a number of times, but it had never hurt this much. It wasn't even dusk yet but she already wished they could have stopped long ago. Her bottom was sore, her legs were exhausted and she was awfully hungry.

Groaning softly, Elànde shifted her position for the tenth time in the past hour. Looking at her fingers she could see that they were turning raw from trying desperately to hold onto the dragon's scales. An effort that had proven entirely futile. In the end she was forced to rely solely on her legs to keep her seated atop the dragon. An activity that left every muscle in her legs aching.

Her back, shoulders and arms all hurt as well. The girl had realized only too late that she had been keeping herself tensed up during the entire morning's ride. When they had stopped for lunch she had been chastised by Arisa and told to relax her muscles more. That was a suggestion more easily made than accomplished for the young girl. Every time Arisa stepped in a hole or shifted her direction Elànde was sure that she would topple off.

When they had started out in the morning she had promised herself she would not be a burden to the dragon. It was foolish but she had believed she could go all day since she would not be the one walking.

It had not taken her long to realize that was not going to be the case.

"Will we be stopping for the night soon?"

They had not spoken much throughout the day. Elànde was unsure how to talk to such a large and impressive animal. In the back of her mind she played out scenarios where she would anger the great beast. All the big men and women from her village always seemed to be angry about something. When compared to this dragon she was with those angry people seemed small.

Every time she asked a question or made a comment Arisa would take a deep breath and exhale it completely before answering. Her responses always left Elànde feeling like the discussion was closed.

This time was certainly no different when the answer finally came after some delay.

"The sun has not yet drawn near the horizon."

Well, there was almost no difference this time. In truth she did not think she could manage to stay seated any longer without losing her legs entirely. Mustering her courage she tried one more time.

"I am so tired. I don't think I can keep going any longer."

Arisa was quiet for some time before answering. Elànde began to worry she was right in thinking the discussion had already been closed.

After a number of steps the dragon finally answered.

"If you can manage just a little bit longer then I will begin looking for a place to stop for the night."

Elànde managed a small smile before giving her thanks. She was relieved that Arisa was willing to stop. In fact she believed that her muscles even relaxed just a little bit at hearing those words.

"Yes, I think I can make it. Thank you."

After another ten minutes or so, which seemed an eternity to Elànde, Arisa finally stopped. After looking around at their surroundings for a bit she announced their arrival.

"We will stay here for the night. You may get down now."

She had been excited at the prospect of stopping and being able to get down. However, Elànde suddenly realized that she would have to actually get down off the dragon. When they stopped briefly for lunch it had been hard enough to not fall flat on her face while climbing down. Now that she was even more tired she was sure she would do just that.

There was nothing for it, though. She just had to manage with as much strength as her tired arms and legs could provide.

"Did you hear me up there? I said you may get down now."

"Yes! Yes, I did. I'm not sure how to get down without falling. My legs are so tired."

After a moment of silence Arisa surprised the girl by carefully laying down. It did not look like it was a very comfortable position for the dragon. The previous night she had lain partly on her side and that had looked much more natural to Elànde. Now she looked much more like a dog that had stretched out in the sun.

"This is as close to the ground as I can get you without knocking you off myself."

"Oh, thank you. I will try to manage from here."

With that Elànde began to edge towards the side and slowly slide down. Half way down her feet set on Arisa's foreleg. She nearly lost her balance at the unexpected stop but managed to hold herself upright before hopping down to the ground.

Arisa waited a moment for the child to move away before standing back up and turning to address her directly.

"Even though you are sore you should spend some time walking around. It will lessen the aches come morning if you do so."

Nodding silently Elànde looked around for a moment, unsure where she should actually walk to. Deciding on small circles she began a slow, painful, march. It hurt to move her legs but it also felt strangely good. After a dozen or so steps her back began to feel better as well. If she was this sore right now she didn't want to think what tomorrow would be like.

* * * * *

During their time traveling through the day Arisa had been unsure how to speak with the small child atop her back. It wasn't that she had never spoken to children before, but in truth it was somewhat uncommon for her. When passing through villages the children were generally too afraid to approach her, let alone speak to her. When they did they were always accompanied by the adults.

Therefore her time in talking to human children was extremely limited. Because of this she had never grown comfortable dealing with them. She simply could not understand how they thought. One minute they would be running around laughing excitedly and the next they were crying uncontrollably because a toy they were playing with had broken.

The small child traveling with her was an even bigger enigma for Arisa to figure out. There was the additional problem that this child had just lost her family and village. Quite possibly every person she had ever known in her short life. Arisa knew she had no way to understand what the child must be feeling. She herself had never formed the kinds of bonds that would lead her to such sadness at their passing. So she had little in her life to help her understand what the girl must be going through. This uncertainty had caused Arisa to remain quiet throughout most of the day.

Every time the child said something she found herself exhaling in frustration. Not because of what the girl had said. Rather because Arisa did not know how to answer safely. She was worried that she might say something to set the girl off crying, and that was something she simply did not know how she would handle.

In the end, it had been a very quiet day for both of them. Arisa felt uncomfortable in the silence, but it was the lesser of the evils. Now that darkness had fallen the pair sat in front of a small fire made from wood gathered by the child and lit by her own fiery breath. It was obvious the girl was finally thinking about her family while she stared into the fire.

After a time, the girl switched her gaze to the dragon lying on the other side of the fire from her. It was evident, even to Arisa, that with nothing to do but let her mind wander she was now thinking of the things and people that had been lost. Or perhaps, taken from her.

"Why did everyone die?"

Arisa met the girl's sad eyes with a rather uncomfortable feeling showing in her own eyes. She had been considering all day how to have this discussion once the human was ready, but even still she was unsure what to say.

"Oh child, I do not know."

After a brief pause Arisa mustered her own courage and continued with something she hoped would help.

"There are questions we may simply never know the answer to. All we can do is move forward and try to continue living."

"But you were there, don't you know what caused the fire?"

"I am sorry, but I do not. I do not remember arriving at your village, nor do I remember what caused me to crash into the building you found me in."

"You don't?"

"No. The last thing I remember is flying through the clouds. From the shape of the moon last night it must have been only a few days ago. After that I remember nothing until you awoke me. In all likelihood whatever happened that caused me to end up unconscious in that building also caused me to forget my memories of the past few days."

Arisa eyed the child with concern. She was staring into the fire with troubled thoughts written on her face, it was some time before she again spoke to the dragon.

"Did… you start the fire?"

"I—I do not know. But I believe it could not have been me. I have never had any ill will towards any humans so I cannot believe that I would have had anything to do with what happened to your village."

She considered the child's face before continuing.

"I have visited many villages and spent much time with your kind and have never had any desire to cause harm. Many villages have offered me shelter and food in exchange for my services. I have no way to prove to you, or to myself, that it was not me, other than reminding you of our current situation. If I truly intended harm to your people would I be helping you now?"

Sad eyes looked down at the ground before quietly answering.

"No."

"I am unsure why I was at your village at all. But it is certainly possible that your village caught on fire for some other reason. We dragons have keen vision so I may have seen the fire and come to help. If I was caught in the building when it collapsed it is possible that the debris rendered me unconscious."

Arisa did not feel good about her answer. She felt somewhat deceitful as she knew there was no way she would have just walked into that building. The damage to the wall was clearly caused by her crashing into it uncontrolled. However, she knew not how to explain this to the child in the current situation.

"Then, why am I the only one to survive? Where did everybody else go?"

"Those are things that trouble me as well, child. I could find no signs that anybody had escaped. Neither the night of the fire nor the morning after. What is also troubling is that there was no sign that anybody had died in the village either. It is as if the village was empty before the fire started."

"But—"

The girl could not do more than mutter that single word. Sighing softly, Arisa tried to put her thoughts into words that the child would comprehend.

"I know. I understand that people were in the village with you that night. But I am at a loss to explain it. There was no sign of bodies, nor were there signs that anyone had fled. Anyway I cannot believe your parents would have left you behind. It is as if they just vanished altogether."

Elànde remained quiet.

"I know this is difficult for you to understand, but I have no better way to explain it."

"Then what will happen to me?"

"You will live on. I will remain with you until we find a village and somebody to take care of you. I will not leave you behind until I am sure that you will be safe."

"Will I ever see you again after you leave?"

"I am sure you will. I promise that I will come back and check on you whenever I am flying in this part of the land."

The girl sniffed slightly but looked happy at hearing those words. Arisa wondered just how often she would be visiting this child. It wasn't as if she kept to a fixed route in her travels, she simply went wherever she felt like going at the time. It may have been be an empty promise to make. However, it was probably best not to mention that to the girl just yet. After being with others of her kind for a short period of time she would likely forget about Arisa. Hoping to change the subject Arisa addressed the girl again.

"Tell me child, the bracelet you wear, why

were you wearing it the night we met? Would it not be uncomfortable to sleep with that around your arm?"

The girl touched the bracelet on her arm and remained quiet a moment for responding.

"It... was a gift from my mother. She said I should always wear it and that if I did it would keep me safe. She told me to never take it off no matter what."

Groaning inwardly at her utter failure, Arisa wracked her brain for something she could say that would not make things worse.

"I see. Well I suppose we must say that it worked. Whatever happened at the village it seems to have done its job and kept you safe."

The great dragon watched the child fiddle with the trinket. It undoubtedly brought her a mixture of fond memories and sad memories at the same time.

"It is getting late. You should try to sleep. We will be leaving in the morning at first light."

Elànde nervously looked around beyond the light of the fire.

"What if a wild animal comes?"

Arisa snorted loudly. Such a ridiculous question to ask a dragon.

"And what wild animals do you think might come that would cause any harm to you?"

"Aren't there bears?"

Arisa gave the child a smile, perhaps a bit more chilling than intended.

"Do you think a bear could manage to stand up against me? Truly what bear would even think to approach you with me nearby? Animals hunt prey that is easy to obtain, they would not bother to try and take something from me."

"You won't go anywhere during the night?"

"Rest assured little one, I will not."

Elànde stood up and walked over to where the dragon laid upon the ground.

"Can I sleep next to you like I did last night?"

"Am I not uncomfortable to sleep against?"

Arisa couldn't imagine the girl wanting to sleep against her scales. Dragons were considered beautiful to look at, but their scales were somewhat rough to the touch.

"You're warm."

"Hmm. So I am just a warming rock for you to sleep near, is that it? Well you should be glad that I breath fire and can remain warm well into the night. Very well. You may sleep against my side again to stay warm. But I will caution you, I take no responsibility for your safety while sleeping that way. I am liable to squash you if I were to roll over."

Sensing the joke in Arisa's words the girl smiled before she responded.

"Thank you."

* * * * *

It had been four days of travel before the child had begun to complain about hunger and water in earnest. Before leaving the village they had managed to find a few water skins and a bag to store some extra carrots. Their time had not been filled with conversation, but one of their short talks had yielded the name of the child's village.

If Arisa not been with her the girl probably would have drank all the water long ago. As it was the dragon forced her to ration what food and water they had. Since then another two days had passed. Now six days into their journey even Arisa had begun to worry about finding another village.

Despite not needing food or water herself nearly as often, even Arisa began to feel the affects of not eating or drinking. She knew she could last awhile still, but that did not mean she did not feel the pain of hunger or thirst. Arisa was also acutely aware that the child was thirsty and hungry for more than just carrots. Food aside, if they did not find water soon she was concerned the child would fall gravely ill.

"I'm tired, can we stop and rest?"

They had only been traveling a few short hours. If the child was complaining this early in the day it did not bode well for being able to continue their journey until dark.

"We cannot. I know you are tired but we must keep going."

"But…"

The child sniffed softly before continuing.

"What if we went the wrong way? What if I didn't remember right?"

Dragons themselves did not whine. To be more specific, they were not really capable of making the rather annoying sound that went along with the action. However, just because she could not make the sounds herself, Arisa was certainly able to recognize a whine when she heard one. And this child was performing the routine with expertise.

"Complaining about it will not change matters any. We have chosen this direction and it is too late to change our minds and go back. We must simply continue until we find the village. If we have gone the wrong way then we shall certainly find something. This path we are following is fairly well travelled and must be here for a reason. It will surely lead us somewhere."

Elànde was quiet. Too quiet for the dragon to think all was well with her.

Despite the earlier whining it was obvious to Arisa that the child was truly afraid they might perish.

"Do you believe me?"

"I- don't know."

"Do you believe *in* me then?"

"In you?"

"Yes. To believe *in* someone is to have faith in their ability to protect you. To trust that they will watch over you and be honest with you. So, do you believe *in* me? Do you believe that I will be truthful to you?"

"I guess so."

"Hmph. Not the unwavering answer I would

have liked to hear from you. Do you lack faith in my *ability* to protect you?"

"No."

"Then you must not believe that I *will* watch over you?"

"I do."

"Well, you must not believe that I will always be honest and truthful with you since that is all that is left. I must say that hurts my pride to be told by a child that they think I would not be truthful to them."

"No, that's not it!"

Arisa smirked softly. Too quietly for the child to have heard it. She was by no means an expert in children now, but the past few days with the child had helped her understand how to deal with this particular girl somewhat.

"I cannot describe how hurtful it is to be told by someone that they think you are a liar. In forty years I have never been called a liar. I have traded with villages, conversed with other dragons, even dealt with those that intend harm. In all that time none have ever dared call me a liar, but now a small child tells me she does not believe me to be truthful. How this wounds me."

It took much effort but Arisa managed to suppress the quiver of laughter that longed to run through her.

"I didn't say you were lying!"

"Then – do you believe *in* me? Do you have faith in my ability to protect you? Do you trust me to be truthful with you?"

Elànde was quiet for a moment before giving her answer.

"Yes, I do."

"Then, when I say that we will survive, do you believe me?"

"I… will try."

"Hmph. I suppose that is a sta—"

Arisa abruptly stopped speaking and walking. It was enough to throw Elànde completely off balance but she managed to hold on and right herself.

"What happened? Why did—"

"Shh!"

Arisa looked off to the left and focused on the soft sounds coming from that direction.

"I hear something."

"What d—"

"Shush child!"

After a moment Arisa spoke again to the child.

"I am going to start running, off to the left. You will need to watch carefully and hold on tight."

"A-alright."

Elànde squeezed her legs and did her best to grab hold of a scale in each hand.

"Here we go."

* * * * *

The dragon started with a jog for a few paces. Even that was enough to cause Elànde to fear losing her balance. She tightened her grip even further. As if she had been waiting for just that action, Arisa took off at a full run.

On and on they ran. It seemed like an eternity that they ran through the forest. Elànde could not believe the speed the dragon was capable of. Darting through the trees so quickly that the scenery became just a blur to her. She tried to look to the side to see how close they were to the trees as they whizzed past but that only made her sick.

Occasionally Elànde could feel the edge of a tree branch brush past her legs. Because of the speed it felt like she was being hit with a switch. Actually, being hit with a switch might have hurt less. After some time she could feel a trickle of blood begin to run down her right leg, though she dared not reach down to feel.

"Hang on!"

The dragon's sudden shout startled Elànde but she managed to respond to the command and gripped as tightly as she could. The next moment brought forth a terrible sensation. Her stomach suddenly felt like it was no longer where it was supposed to be. She was also vaguely aware that the thudding of Arisa's feet could not longer be heard.

Before she could open her mouth to scream she lurched forward and heard the impact of Arisa's feet hitting the ground again. Although she slid sideways at the jolt from the landing, Elànde managed to just keep herself from falling off completely. Along with the sound of feet crashing onto the ground she heard the cry of an animal and then nothing but the sound of Arisa's labored breathing.

"Wha… What happened?"

"We have dinner. That is what has happened."

Even before seeing the deer on the ground she understood what Arisa meant. There on the ground was the dead animal. It had several long cuts on it's side from the dragon's claws. Elànde looked more closely to try and tell what kind of animal it was.

She immediately decided it had been a mistake to be curious of such a thing. The wounds from the dragon's claws were not the only damage the animal had sustained. There was also the distinct, if not disturbing, fact that the back half of the animal was somewhat flatter than the front half. Likely from one of Arisa's heavy feet.

"I want you to climb down and gather some wood for a fire, we will need to cook the flank for you to be able to eat it. I am going to look for water. The deer would not travel very far from a source of water, so there should be something nearby."

"Okay. You won't go far?"

Arisa sighed softly while the child slithered down.

"No, I will not go far."

* * * * *

Once Elànde was on solid ground and gathering wood, somewhat away from the dead animal, Arisa moved off in search of the water source. If there was indeed water nearby she should be able to hear it and smell it once she got far enough away from the odor of fresh blood.

As she moved off she looked back at the young girl gathering wood and noticed her slightly limping. Looking at her leg more closely she could see it was bleeding slightly. In fact both legs had red welts all over them. She turned away again and continued her trek to find water to drink, and now to clean the wounds on the child's legs.

Arisa felt bad about causing the girl pain. While running she hadn't considered that the child didn't have any scales to protect her against the tree branches. Through that entire sprint Arisa hadn't heard her cry out even once.

"Hmm."

There was indeed water nearby, she could hear it. It was faint, but it was surely there. Arisa listened carefully until she felt sure she knew which direction it was and then moved off towards the sound. After a few minutes of walking she spotted the stream.

Calling it a stream was a bit of an exaggeration, it was only a trickle of water. However, there were a few small pools that it travelled through, and they were clean. It would provide enough water for them to continue for a while, especially with the meat they were about to eat.

Arisa went back for her small companion. In another thirty minutes time they had both drank their fill of water and were waiting for the meat to finish cooking.

"You have done this before?"

"Yes, my father took me hunting sometimes."

"Then you have seen animals killed for food before?"

Arisa was somewhat curious why the child had seemed to avoid the carcass if she had seen dead animals before.

"Yes, but... They have always been killed by a single arrow when I have seen them before. I have never seen a deer killed... like that."

"Ah."

Nodding at her short explanation, Arisa considered what the child said. It was a common thing for herself to see, and even be the one causing, an animal to be torn apart. It was just part of being a dragon. But for the young girl sitting between her front legs it was indeed probably a new experience.

They were resting in front of the fire while they waited. Arisa had stretched herself out, curling partway around the fire. The girl was using one of her scaled legs as a pillow while poking at the fire with a long stick.

"Do your legs still hurt, child?"

"A little. But it's not so bad now."

After starting the fire they had gone to where Arisa had found the water and filled up the skins. They both took their fill of water as well before

Elànde washed the wounds on her legs. Once cleaned up her legs did not look as bad as they did at first, but Arisa still felt uneasy for causing the child pain.

"I am sorry for damaging you. I should have been more attentive to what I was doing and the consequences it would have on you."

"No, it's okay. It hurt, but you were trying to get food for us."

Elànde got up to carefully turn the steak over using a pair of sticks. While up she checked on her legs one more time. There were still obvious welts but the pain was mostly gone.

Arisa watched her small companion. The warmth from the human girl was insignificant compared to that of the fire, or even that generated by her own body. Even so she keenly noticed the absence of warmth when the girl got up. As Elànde settled back into her spot it surprised Arisa that she would find it so comforting to have the child near her.

"You did very well today. When we were running you held on and kept your place upon my back. I am very proud of you."

"I was surprised when you started running."

"I should have told you what was happening, I am sorry. But I did not want to risk the deer fleeing before I could go into motion myself. It was hard enough to catch up to it as it was."

"No, it's okay. I was just surprised. I didn't know you could run so fast."

Arisa snorted loudly.

"I should be able to run much faster, but I am out of shape. Dragons do not normally travel on the ground in such manner. We are creatures of flight and the muscles for flight are what I have trained. My legs are not used to such exertion."

"How much faster can you fly?"

"Hmm. I do not know. I am not accustomed to judging distances from the ground. However, I believe I could have flown in a single day the distance we have walked thus far with daylight to spare."

"That fast?"

"Yes. And when traveling alone I do not normally stop at sundown. I can see well enough to continue flying well into the dark of the night."

Arisa looked over at the campfire and sniffed the air.

"I believe your lunch is ready to pull some off."

"Oh!"

Elànde scrambled to retrieve the meat that was beginning to burn. In her haste she neglected to use the sticks she had used a moment ago and singed her fingers trying to grab the meat from the fire.

"Ouch!"

"Be careful."

Arisa stretched her leg out and pierced the steak with one of her claws. She drew it out of the fire and placed it on a rock within reach of the child.

Elànde carried the makeshift plate back to her spot by the dragon's side. Leaning back against her while slowly picking at the cooling meat she smiled up at Arisa.

"Thank you."

"Well, we cannot have you burning your fingers off. If would be most difficult for you to climb up onto my back later if you did so. Now eat up. You will need to eat more than you feel you can. We do not know how much farther we must travel."

The two rested in silence while Elànde slowly ate her steak. It took some effort to find the edible parts. Neither was skilled in cooking so some parts were well charred while other spots were undercooked. It was, however, a large steak so there was plenty of meat to fill the child up.

Elànde was finally coming to the end of her meal. She had been moaning through each bite for the past few minutes but continued to eat at Arisa's prompting. The dragon suddenly lifted her head and looked off in the distance.

"What is it?"

Arisa did not respond but instead twitched her head slightly to the side.

"There is something out there."

"Another deer?"

"I do not believe so. I think… I think it may be other humans."

"Really!?"

"Come. Gather your things and climb up. We will investigate and hope for the best."

The girl scurried around to gather the water skins into her bag before clambering back up the dragon. While she did this Arisa carefully stomped out the fire. Over the past few days Elànde had become accustomed as to how best to climb up the dragon quickly without causing either of them great discomfort. Although her bottom did protest at once again having to sit atop the hard scales.

"I'm ready."

"Then let us be off."

Arisa moved off at a light jog. She remembered the child's wounds and was careful to more fully avoid the trees around them. As soon as she began moving she could feel Elànde tighten her grip and hunker down for the faster movement.

As they moved through the forest Arisa changed her direction numerous times whenever she caught a trace of sound or scent. She had hope because of the difficulty in finding the exact direction to travel. This meant either village hunters out gathering food, or possibly bandits. The chance of the latter was rather small. Marauders would not normally try so hard to conceal themselves unless they were about to attack others.

Arisa was still considering the remote possibility of needing to flee in a hurry when they finally caught sight of the humans. A sigh of relief escaped her upon seeing them. It was obvious with only a brief look to tell that these were hunters and not bandits. She would finally get the small child somewhere safe.

Slowing her pace, Arisa approached the hunters. She could already see that they were aware of her presence. They were obviously cautious of her as they remained mostly hidden in the brush . She could hardly blame them. It was not likely they expected to meet a large dragon wandering through the forest on the ground. As she got closer they stepped out from the underbrush into the open and hailed her.

"Hallo there! Do you come peacefully?"

"We do. I have with me a human child. We seek the nearest village so that the child may be among her own kind. I am Arisa, daughter of Tirza, the child here is named Elànde, daughter of Marlene."

The hunters looked up at the child and considered the situation. It was very possible they had never seen a dragon traipsing through the woods. Let alone a human child riding atop a dragon. Arisa was positive that she had never seen such a sight herself.

"Where is the child from?"

By now Arisa had arrived in front of the hunters and crouched down to allow Elànde to climb down. It also allowed Arisa to speak to the hunters on the same level. She did not want to frighten them in such an unusual situation.

"She comes from a village away to the south. called…"

Arisa was suddenly aware that she did not actually know the name of the village. She had never bothered to ask Elànde what her home had been called. It couldn't be helped, she would just have to ask now."

"Elànde, what was the name of your village?"

It took the child a moment to look up and respond to Arisa.

"Konsau."

The hunter who spoke a moment ago took a step forward from the others.

"What has happened to bring you here?"

Arisa glanced at the child, who was leaning heavily against her flank. Cowering away slightly from the hunters, it was apparent that Elànde was not going to be doing much more talking to these strangers.

"Her family is gone. Along with the rest of the village. We do not know what happened. Only that it was destroyed by fire and there were no other survivors besides her. The rest of the story is best saved for a later time."

"I understand. Please allow us to speak apart for a moment."

The spokesman turned around and began discussing with the others. Arisa found it humorous that they apparently believed she could not hear their whispered conversation. It seems they were trying to decide what to do. They did not believe that the entire hunting party should return to the village so they were trying to decide who would lead them back.

The spokesman of the group turned back.

"The elders will have more questions for you once you reach the village. For now, Kale will guide you back and bring you before the elders. It is but half a days walk from here. You should be there shortly before nightfall. The rest of us must continue hunting."

"We give you our gratitude."

Arisa nodded her head. Using her best etiquette possible, she addressed Kale directly.

"I understand what it means to abandon the hunt. We appreciate that you make this sacrifice for our welfare. I shall endeavor to repay you in kind once things are settled and my wing has healed."

The one named Kale bowed before turning to lead them further away from the path they had originally been on.

"Please, come this way. We must travel around the hunting grounds so as to not scare the game from the rest of the hunting party."

"We shall follow your lead."

Turning to the small child at her side, Arisa continued.

"Elànde, we are in the hunting grounds of others, so we must both travel as quietly as we may until Kale tells us it is safe. We are guests in this land and we must treat their land and their laws with respect. I am sure we have already scared enough game away to cause them difficulty. Now, climb up and we shall be off."

The girl nodded without a word and

scampered up her protector's side. Arisa saw the eyes of the hunters widen at seeing the child crawling up and sitting atop a great dragon.

It was true that they had already seen Elànde sitting upon her back. Still, it hadn't occurred to her when she told the girl to crawl up that she now had an audience watching. It was rather humiliating for her but she tried to ignore it. There was still absolutely no grace in the way the girl clambered up.

"Kale, please lead the way and we shall remain as quiet as we may."

CHAPTER 4

"Then Konsau is destroyed?"

Arisa stood before the elders and many of the villagers in the town square. As they travelled their guide had explained to them that it was called Rupsê. She had just finished explaining what had transpired to bring them both here. Normally this type of conversation would have taken place in private so the elders could tell the rest of the villagers in their own way. However, due to her size, there was no other place to hold such a meeting.

"Yes. There is nothing left. No building, animal or person has survived except for the girl."

The girl, Elànde, was off with a few of the wives being tended to. It took some convincing to get her to leave the dragon but in the end she had gone. Arisa did not want her around to hear, once again, about the destruction of her village.

"And you truly have no knowledge of what brought about this destruction?"

"I do not. Whether it be from the crash into the building or some other force my memory only goes back to when I was awoken by the child. Unless there is a greater gap in my memory, the last thing I remember is five days since the last moon."

"Hmm."

"The last large city I remember visiting was Narùt. Can you tell me, have you heard of it and how far it might be?"

"Yes, it is nearby. Or rather, it would be considered near to a dragon. I believe it would take you but six days to reach it."

"Then I believe my accounting of time is true. I have lost only half a cycle of the moon. After Narùt I made only one stop at a small village before my memory failed. I do not believe I would have spent so much time in this area to have lost an entire cycle of the moon."

"What of the girl, does she know what happened?"

"She does not. Elànde has told me that she remembers only awaking to the fire at night and not being able to find her parents. It was while she was still looking for her parents that I, evidently, crashed into her village. However…"

Arisa hesitated and glanced at the gathered villagers. She did not like having to say what was on her mind in such a public place, but she had no way to tell them privately.

"… due to the lack of bodies, or any other signs of escape, I cannot rule out the possibility of magic."

There were small gasps throughout the gathered crowed. The elders themselves looked uncomfortable at the mention of the word. One finally cleared his throat and spoke loudly to be heard over the crowd. He had introduced himself as Katarr at their arrival a few minutes ago.

"But there has not been evidence of a true

magic user in over three hundred years. Only in hearsay and rumor has magic been talked about."

"I do not say that it was for sure magic. Only that it might be possible. We dragons live long lives, and our memories are without flaw. The stories of those days are passed down from one generation to the next in perfect detail."

In light of her own amnesia such a statement suddenly made Arisa uncomfortable.

"We dragons remember things you do not. I am young yet, even by the reckoning of my kin, but I have spoken with others of my kind who remember when magic was widely in use. It is true that all traces were eradicated, but that does not mean it can never return. Please understand me, I must stress that I am not saying it was magic. Just that I must consider it a possibility under the circumstances."

Ketarr, nodded and once again spoke up to be heard over the murmurs of the crowd.

"We understand. We have no reason to doubt the story of the dragon Arisa who stands before us. We will send a number of hunters to scout the village of Konsau to be sure it is indeed the one they have travelled from. You should all return to your own homes. We will discuss Konsau no further for the time being. For now we must discuss what to do with the child. Please, go back to your own tasks."

The crowd continued to murmur for a short time but slowly disbanded regardless. After most of the villagers had moved away Arisa returned her attention to Ketarr and shared her own regret.

"I am sorry to have caused you grief by bringing such news."

"Let your sorrow be felt for those who have perished. We must discuss what is to be done now. You are not the first dragon to visit us so I believe we can make some preparations for your stay. I expect you will need to wait for your wing to heal before continuing on your own journey?"

"Yes. However... the child has grown attached to me. I have made a promise to her to remain with her until she is safe and..."

The elder looked upon her with keen interest. It was the first time he had opportunity to see a dragon look so uncomfortable.

"Yes?"

"I believe I may have become somewhat attached to her as well. I would like to stay until I am sure that she is safe and well taken care of. I also feel that I should not depart until she gives me leave to do so."

"I see. Is your concern that she may not give such leave?"

"No, but I fear it may be much longer than would be agreeable for you. I believe it would cause grief for your village if I were to remain here for much longer than it takes my injury to heal."

Ketarr smiled at the concerned dragon before responding.

"Let not such worries trouble you. As I said, you are not the first dragon to visit us. We have had a few in my lifetime. It will not be an inconvenience for us to make accommodations for you during your stay. Let us deal with the immediate concerns of the child's, as well as your own, care and safety. We can leave other matters to be decided when those are finished."

"In any case, I offer my gratitude. I shall repay your kindness once I am rested."

"To my mind, you have already repaid what kindness we shall show you by the kindness you have shown that young girl. It could not have been convenient for you to have brought that child all this way. Dragons have always been honest and trustworthy. But even so, I believe many would have left the child and simply told the nearest village where she could be found."

Arisa did not know what to say. Before she could summon an appropriate response the old man continued.

"In truth it may have been faster to leave her at the village and move at your full speed. But I have no doubt that the child would have come to more harm by such an action, even if just to her heart. For now, we shall make room for you in the horse stable. I am told by your fellow dragons that once cleaned and lined with fresh straw, it makes for a comfortable place to rest."

"I thank you for your kindness. What shall you do with the girl?"

"I will speak with the others and try to find a home for her. For now, she may stay with my wife and me. It has been many years since we have had children but we still have a bed she may sleep in until something more permanent can be found."

"Once again, I thank you."

"Now let us attend to your injuries. The girl is being cared for but you are in need of some attention yourself. We have some herbs and ointments that we apply to burns, although you do not have skin as we do. It has been many days since your injury but they may still be of some assistance to your healing."

Arisa nodded and opened her mouth to speak, but was cut off before she could answer.

"And do not thank us once again. It is a waste of time that could be spent tending to your wounds."

The elders had left Arisa in the care of a number of the ladies of the village. They had carefully cleaned and dressed the burned wing while the men prepared the stable for her to rest in.

It was true. The stable was quite comfortable. The horses were none too happy at having their home usurped by another. However, they did seem satisfied to be put out to pasture once they saw the hulking dragon moving in their direction.

It had already been dusk when they had arrived in the village. Speaking with the elders had taken some time and it was past mealtime once they had finished. Arisa tried to convince the wives that her injury was fine and would heal itself and that they should return to their families to prepare the meal. She had not met with success.

It was now nearly midnight and she was lying comfortably on a bed of straw. It was one of the great joys she had in visiting villages. She always made every effort to not have anyone go out of their way on her account. But the villagers were always happy to allow her the use of straw to sleep on. A very pleasant change from sleeping out in the wild where she often had to sleep on rocks, or ground wet from the rains.

As she basked in the wonderful feeling of being able to finally rest she heard the creak of a door opening. What followed was the sounds of hesitant footsteps. And a smell she had become quite familiar with over the past week. Without the need to open her eyes Arisa spoke softly to Elànde.

"You should be in bed, child."

"I can't sleep."

"Nor can I when one is sneaking around me at night."

"I'm sorry."

Arisa opened her eyes and looked upon the girl in the darkness of the stable.

"Why can you not sleep?"

"I'm cold."

"Did you not have a soft, warm bed to sleep in?"

"Yes."

"Then why can you not sleep?"

"It's too quiet."

"What?"

"When I sleep next to you I can hear your heart. It reminds me of my mother holding me close when I would have nightmares."

"Ahh, I see. Very well. But you cannot make a habit of coming out here to sleep with me. You must learn to sleep on your own again."

The girl nodded enthusiastically, "Then I can stay?"

"Yes, child, you may stay and sleep with me. It may not be as comfortable as a bed, but it should at least be more comfortable than the hard ground we have slept on these past few nights."

* * * * *

"But why can't I go with you?"

"I am not going far, child. I will only be gone at most an hour. And I shall be flying, that is why you cannot go. I must see if my wing has healed properly. It has been nearly a whole cycle of the moon since I have flown. I must strengthen my wings again."

It had taken far longer for her wing to heal than Arisa thought, even with the ointments the villagers had continued to put on her. The heat from the fire had passed completely through her scales and burnt the soft underside of her wing. Finally, the village healer had pronounced her fit to fly. Her flesh had healed well, but the color of the scales on her wing might well retain a scorched look forever.

"But I want to go with you."

"You cannot fly yourself so you cannot go with me."

"Can't I ride on your back?"

Arisa tried to ignore the guffaws of the villagers who were watching their exchange. Elànde had joined her on walks, usually with the girl riding atop her back. It still provided awe and humor to the villagers to see them together like that. None of the animals in the village were too keen on having a large dragon walking around them so she had taken many walks outside the village, usually accompanied by Elànde.

"No. You have enough difficulty staying on my back when I am walking unless I tread carefully. There is no way you could manage to stay seated while I am flying."

"You said I was doing good though!"

Now I understand why we dragons leave our hatchlings before they are born. It is so we do not eat our young before they have a chance to grow up.

Arisa replied sharply.

"Listen to me, child. You have done well on my back while I am walking. But even now I walk slowly and carefully so that you do not lose your balance. Even so, if you were to fall from my back you would do little more than bruise yourself. When I am flying I can not fly slowly or even in such a way that you would not lose your balance. And if you fall from me while flying you would be far worse than be bruised."

Crestfallen, Elànde looked at the ground. Arisa felt badly for her but it was simple truth that she could not take the child with her flying.

"I promise I will be back soon."

Elànde made no further attempt to argue for staying with her. Softly she gave a final response.

"Alright."

Arisa stepped away from the child and stretched out her wings to full length. As always, it felt wonderful to feel the sun soak into the thinnest part of her wings. Stretching to the fullest would slightly separate the scales on her wings allowing the heat to soak in deep.

After a few soft flaps to get a feel of her newly healed wing Arisa leapt into the air and flew once again, albeit a bit unsteadily. She found it difficult at first to balance herself. Her right wing was no longer as strong as the left. This forced her to concentrate on her flying, much as she had to do when she had first begun to learn the skill.

She hoped it wasn't too evident from the ground how much trouble she was having. To her, it felt like she was wobbling back and forth all over the sky.

I suppose I might look like a drunk human wandering through the streets at night.

The humans below were already quite small and shrinking steadily away. Even from this distance Arisa could still make out Elànde watching her intently. Much to the dragon's dismay, the girl had grown even more attached to her over the past moon. She assumed the child would want to spend more time with the others of her kind. There were a number of children her own age in the village. Arisa couldn't understand why the child didn't play with her own kind more.

If Arisa was nearby, Elànde would happily play with the other children. Unfortunately, as soon as the dragon began to move off the girl was instantly by Arisa's side, following her wherever she went. It didn't matter that Arisa's task was to talk to the elders, go hunting for food or any other task. The child was instantly by her side.

She had verbally snapped at the child a few times, worse than she had a little while ago. Arisa was happy to be able to spend some time alone, and soaring through the sky was certainly her favorite pastime. The girl had an uncanny ability to get under her scales. Perhaps it was because of all the time they had spent together over the past cycle, she wasn't sure.

The only thing she was convinced about was that it didn't look like she would be leaving the girl behind anytime soon. It wasn't so much that she didn't want to remain in the company of the child. She actually enjoyed being with Elànde. As much as it initially had been degrading to her, she even found herself becoming fond of teaching the girl to ride upon her back. The child learned quickly and seemed to enjoy being challenged.

Arisa had risen to a good altitude and gave herself a rest. She stretched her wings to the fullest and allowed herself to glide through the air. Far below she could see the village and even from this height she could make out many of the villagers she had come to know.

Would it be possible for her to fly with me? I have heard of other dragons carrying the dead for burial, and occasionally even cargo for humans in an emergency. But in all my travels I cannot think of ever hearing of a human riding upon a dragon. It is always possible it may have happened in the past but still…

Having rested her wing while gliding for a while, Arisa began to flap and gain altitude once more.

Even if I were to allow it, is it possible for her to fly with me? No, even with practice it would be too hard for the child to hang on. A single gust of wind or shift in the air currents could knock her off. It is unlikely I would be able to catch her if that were to happen.

* * * * *

From the ground Elànde watched her protector soar through the air. She was little more than a small bird to the eye but the girl followed her every move all the same. Whenever the dragon came low the child watched even more carefully, not wanting to miss a single wing beat.

"'It's a beautiful thing to watch isn't it?"

Surprised at the sudden voice, Elànde looked behind her to find Ketarr standing nearby. He was the one whose house she was sleeping at – usually. She still snuck out every few nights to sleep with

Arisa. Not once had she been chided by him other than to be told to be careful out at night.

His own children were grown and had families of their own now. He and his wife, Marika, had discussed where the child should stay long term and decided that, if she was happy, she could stay with them. They both saw the unusual attachment she had to the dragon and decided to say nothing to dissuade her. As long as she was safe they were happy to let her slip out at night, and what safer place could she be than next to a dragon who had already proven a worthy guardian and protector.

"Yes, she is very beautiful."

Elànde responded absentmindedly, again watching her friend soar through the open sky.

"I heard you talking to Arisa before she left. Don't worry, she will return for sure."

"It isn't that. I know she will come back."

Ketarr looked down at her with a faint smile.

"But?"

"I really do want to fly too. It must be so much fun to fly through the air the way dragons do."

"Aye, I suppose it is. Then you have always wanted to fly such as the dragons do?"

The girl shook her head slowly before responding.

"No, I had never thought of it before meeting Arisa."

"Oh? And what is it that would make a pretty thing such as yourself want to fly?"

"On our way here I was riding on her back while she walked through the forest. She suddenly told me to hold on tight and then ran. It was the first time she had run with me. The wind rushed by so fast it felt... like flying."

"Ahh, and now you want to experience the real thing, is that it?"

"Uh huh."

"Well my dear, I believe Arisa is correct that it would be too dangerous for you to fly with her."

Elànde's shoulders drooped and she took her eyes off her friend to look at the ground beneath her feet.

"For now."

"For now?"

Elànde had shifted her full attention away from the dragon now. The unexpected statement had completely drawn her in.

"There is no doubt she is correct that you would likely fall off if you were to fly with her just now. That dragon cares for you a great deal. I cannot imagine what happened back in Konsau to the both of you. Whatever terrible evil it was there is one bit of good it brought as well. It made the two of you friends."

Ketarr looked up at the dragon soaring in the sky before continuing.

"And friendship with a dragon is not something to take lightly. Dragons do not discard friends when they are no longer convenient the way many humans do. If a dragon names you as friend to them, you can believe it is for life. And no matter what happens she will always be there for you if you have need."

"But what—"

"I have not heard Arisa say as much, but I believe she counts you as a friend in her heart. She would never do anything to harm you intentionally, and it would hurt her to the core of her being if anything she did ever harmed you unintentionally. That is one reason she says no to you flying with her. The other reason is that it is unheard of."

"What do you mean?"

"I have lived long enough to see my children have children of their own. In all that time I have never heard of a human riding atop a dragon, even on the ground as you do. It is a difficult thing to try something new. For humans such as ourselves, we worry that we might make fools of ourselves and be laughed at by those around us, do we not?"

"I guess."

"Then for a dragon it must be of even greater concern to be ridiculed. So it would naturally be very hard for Arisa to consider doing something so strange. She might well believe that if any of her kin discovered that she allowed you to ride on her, even on the ground, they would make fun of her, or worse, avoid her altogether. I believe that would make her quite sad."

Elànde looked down at the ground dejectedly before responding.

"Oh. Do you think it would be better if I

didn't ride her ever again? I don't want her to be sad."

"Hmm. I do not. In fact I think it would cause her grief if you were to stop going with her on walks."

"But if her friends find out…"

"I think she has decided that her friendship with you is worth more to her than what her other friends might say about you riding upon her back. It began out of need from a crisis, on that alone she could defend her actions to other dragons, not that I believe she will need to. And I think there is something we can do about the flying as well."

"Really?"

"Most dragons are very logical creatures. While they still feel emotions the same as us, they consider carefully how to allow those emotions to affect them. So, because she has an emotion of sadness at the thought of you getting hurt by flying with her, she will consider the possibility of that actually happening and decide based on that."

Ketarr looked at the girl for a moment before continuing.

"Right now, that is a very likely outcome. Remember she would feel badly if you got hurt. But if you were to give her logical reasons why there is very little chance of you being hurt, she might well reconsider her decision."

"How do I make her change her mind?"

"Hah. Well first, my dear, remember that you can never *make* a dragon, or any creature for that matter, change its mind. If a horse refuses to go into the stable then no amount of pushing or pulling will make it change its mind. But if you offer a reward, such as some sweet oats, for going into the stable then that horse will reconsider."

Ketarr paused briefly to kneel down next to the girl and give her a wry smile.

"As for Arisa, there are two things you might be able to do that will give her reason to reconsider. The first is patience and practice. The practice comes by continuing to ride with her on her walks. That way you may become even more accustomed to how she moves. With time you will even be able to stay atop her even at her fastest run.

"I believe we can improve your abilities by having you learn to ride the horses as well. I have watched you and Arisa together and it seems she has already given you the basics of riding. While I have not ridden a dragon myself I suspect it is not very much different than riding a horse."

Elànde's mind swirled with all the information she was receiving.

"The *proof* shall come from your time with Arisa. If she sees that you are able to keep your balance no matter what while on the ground, she will be much more likely to reconsider your ability to keep balanced while flying."

"Okay. What about the other thing? You said two things I could do?"

The earlier smile on Ketarr's face slowly changed into a full grin.

"The second will be a present to both of you when you are ready. For now, focus on learning to ride."

Looking back towards the dragon soaring in the sky Elànde nodded slightly.

"There is something else I think you would do well at. And if you are insistent on being able to fly and travel with Arisa it would suit you well in providing for your meals."

"What do you mean?"

"I mean that it would not be right to rely upon Arisa to provide all of your food, you should be able to provide for yourself. With that in mind, I believe learning the bow would suit you rather well. By learning how to hunt animals with the bow you can provide for yourself, and even on occasion provide a meal for your friend."

"You meal kill them? I don't know..."

The older man put his hand on her shoulder before responding.

"It is not about the act of killing. We do not kill an animal simply for sport, we kill when there is need for food. They understand themselves since it is the same with them. A fox catches and kills a rabbit when it needs to eat, not because it wishes to. As long as it is to sustain your own life you should not worry about taking the life of an animal for food."

Elànde nodded softly while looking back up to the sky. Her friend was nothing more than a tiny dot in the sky moving about. Still she continued to watch.

CHAPTER 5

"I still do not think this is a good idea, Marika."

It was a less than a moon before Elànde's fourteenth birthday. The dragon stood in a special structure the villagers had built shortly after their arrival. It had been her home for nearly four years. It was essentially a stable but they had modified the design slightly to more easily allow her to come and go.

She was being measured every which way by Ketarr's wife. Marika finished the measurement from wing to foreleg and stepped away. Finally lowering the wing she had been holding up above Marika's head, Arisa was now able to speak directly to her.

"What if the child were to fall off? Elànde would surely die if I were not able to catch her in time. Even if I caught her before she hit the ground she would likely still receive serious injuries."

Arisa had still not left the village of Rupsê. Every time she brought up the idea of her moving on, even for a short period of time, Elànde would cry out that she couldn't go.

Marika took a moment to note the last measurement in a small book before giving her response to Arisa.

"Elànde is not a child anymore, and you

should stop thinking of her as one. She may still be young, be she is not a *child*. She takes care of herself far better than any of my own children did at her age."

It bothered Arisa that she could not travel around freely. Traveling and learning new things is what her life had been before meeting Elànde. But despite being able to learn only so much at Rupsê, Arisa had enjoyed the quiet life while she was here. She had made many friends in her time at the village. She had even learned many new ways that various types of meat could be cooked for her. It just was not what she wanted to be doing.

Looking down at her notes, Marika began flipping a few pages back and forth. She hadn't exactly answered Arisa's question, but the dragon knew she had no chance of truly getting Marika's attention until she found whatever it was she was looking for.

Over the past half year Arisa had noticed some peculiarities in Elànde and some of the others. Something strange was going on between Ketarr, Marika, and Elànde as well as a few of the other villagers. Try as she might she could not discover what it was they had been plotting. It had frustrated her more than the plotting itself. Even Elànde had stubbornly refused to say anything about what was going on.

Whenever Arisa tried to bring up the subject of what they might be up to, they would all just smile and change the subject. The only bit of information she could obtain was *you'll see soon enough*. However, that all changed last week when the three of them had approached Arisa with their plan. A plan that left her speechless for its obvious madness.

"It will be fine."

Evidently Marika had found what she was looking for in her notes. Her attention briefly returned to the dragon.

"That is why I am measuring you so we can make a harness for you to wear that will allow Elànde to strap in. This way there will no danger of her falling."

Arisa twisted around to look at the older woman as she resumed stretching her measuring line this way and that.

"But even so…"

"Hold still please. Elànde has proven her ability as a skilled rider, even to you, has she not?"

The dragon shifted uncomfortably. She felt cornered by what Marika said but knew it was her own fault for not outright dismissing this ridiculous idea in the first place.

"Yes, I suppose she has. But if something were to go wrong then—"

Having finished the measurements, Marika walked around to address the dragon face to face.

"Is it the safety of the child you are concerned about or your own pride as a dragon?"

Chagrinned, Arisa looked away.

"I suppose, both."

"Tell me then, how would this affect your pride?"

She didn't want to look the woman in the eye. Arisa knew where this was going. She did not have an answer that satisfied even herself so she did not expect it to satisfy Marika either. Her own pride had always been something she struggled with.

"Being seen by other dragons with Elànde upon my back would shame me in their eyes."

"Do you know for certain, or is that simply what you believe?"

Arisa remained quiet. It was a belief only, but one that she had held for most of her life. Dragons were supposed to be regal creatures. They were beautiful to look upon as well as highly intelligent. Ever dignified, Arisa always strove to exemplify how she… how she believed dragons should behave. Understanding her reason for remaining quiet, Marika continued her questioning.

"Is it possible that other dragons would simply be shocked at seeing something new rather than looking down upon you? Have you ever asked another dragon what they thought of a human riding upon a dragon's back?"

"No. I suppose I have never asked."

"Perhaps humans don't ride dragons because they have never developed a close bond with one. You and Elànde I believe have such a friendship. Maybe you and she will be the first to fly together. Would that be such a bad thing?"

Arisa considered their discussion for a

moment before slowly replying.

"I suppose I will have to continue to give it some thought."

The older woman smiled up at the dragon.

"Ketarr and I love that girl dearly, as if she were one of our own. If we believe it is possible for the two of you to safely do this, then trust that it will be so. As for your pride, you alone must determine if your pride is greater than your friendship with Elànde."

Marika patted Arisa's neck as she opened her notebook and pulled out her measuring tape once again.

"Now, while you think upon those things I must work through these measurements."

Arisa shuffled her feet slightly while Marika made her way towards the door. It was true she had learned to trust both Ketarr and Marika over the years, but it was equally true she had her pride as a dragon to overcome as well. Allowing the child to ride on her back while traveling to this village had been necessary. In those circumstances it was easier for her to allow it.

Even after that she had eventually allowed the girl to continue riding around on her back while on the ground. It would be easy to avoid being seen by other dragons, but up in the air flying between villages was a different matter.

Calling out to the Marika just before she reached the door, Arisa asked one final question of the older lady.

"You will do your best to make it comfortable for me to wear? I would not want to deal with something that scratches up my scales even more. As it is, the proper color has not returned to the scales on my right side. I would not wish to compound that by blemishing them further."

Arisa was looking at the scales on her side which were now permanently singed black. She had hoped that, over time, her burned scales would return to their rightful color but over the years it became clear that would not happen.

"Do not worry my friend. I shall make it so comfortable you will want to sleep in it."

The dragon's shoulders drooped slightly upon hearing that remark.

"I am not sure that makes me feel any better about wearing such a contraption."

The older woman chuckled as she left through the smaller door. Arisa gazed at her surroundings. The humans had done a good job making something comfortable for her to live in. Knowing the girl secretly slept out here from time to time Ketarr even had them put in a bed for Elànde to sleep on. Not that she ever used it. The nights she would sneak out to sleep with Arisa were spent lying against the dragon's side or using one of her forelegs as a pillow.

She knew they cared for the young girl and would never allow anything to bring her harm. It still did not make it any easier for Arisa to accept such an absurd idea. Even if it did not bother her personally the child might still be in danger. If she lost her balance or slipped it would be the end of her.

Still...

Arisa pondered the child's abilities. It was true Elànde had done very well at riding. Over the past few years she had practiced nearly every day riding the various horses in the village. By now she could ride even the most stubborn and ill-mannered horses without much trouble. During all that time she had also learned to fall quite superbly without harming herself.

Even now the girl was out riding in the forest. To Arisa's initial surprise, the girl had taken up and excelled at the bow. At only fourteen many in the village considered her an accomplished archer. She was rather tall for a girl, but her slender features and chestnut colored hair allowed her to easily blend into the forest around her when hunting.

Arisa herself had, after some time, agreed to allow the girl to ride upon her back at times when walking or running to and fro. She still went out flying by herself quite often. Elànde had to accept staying behind those times, but they both enjoyed just walking together and talking. Sometimes they walked side-by-side and other times Arisa did the walking and Elànde simply rode upon her back.

The girl truly enjoyed talking to the dragon. She had very few insights to offer, but she did so enjoy hearing about all the places Arisa had been. Now that she was getting older Elànde was even beginning to enjoy discussing more advanced things. The pair had spent many late nights talking about the sciences and various religious beliefs that Arisa had learned of over her lifetime.

The more they discussed the more Arisa's enjoyment of their talks grew. It was strange, but she had begun to find that her discussions with the child were more interesting than when she spoke with others in the village. The fact that the child had gotten to know her very well over the years and knew how to get under her scales was likely part of it. Elànde could occasionally find small holes in Arisa's logic. Even though it irked the dragon, she found trying to talk her way out of those times a challenge to be relished.

Even the times they talked about the users of magic from years past the child made every effort to keep up. She remembered well what had been discussed previously and would bring it up herself when it related to the current topic. Arisa always endeavored to not scare the child, but she did not want to shield her from the truth of what those who used magic were capable of.

Sigh. Why did I ever agree to this in the first place? I could have just said no to Elànde. She would have gotten over it I am sure. If I could have just managed to not let them get me flustered I would have been able to fend off their arguments.

They had grouped up on her. And they had planned their attack carefully. Every single time she brought up a reason to say *no* they had an argument ready to counter her. In the end she had become nervous and began to stutter out any excuse she could think of. Even those they had been prepared for. Finally she had agreed to reserve final judgement until after they had finished the harness and had a chance to test it.

The problem was, she could not think of any way out of this if the harness worked as expected. It wasn't as if she *wanted* them to fail. She just could think of no other way out of this predicament. And this contraption would be far closer to being… a saddle.

Arisa sighed once more and then slowly made her way outside. She couldn't think straight and wanted to go for a flight to clear her head. Flying through the air always helped her gather her thoughts. She nudged the giant doors open with her nose and stepped out into the sun.

"Ahh. The sun always feels so good in this part of the world."

The dragon closed her eyes and stretched her wings out as far as she could. She wanted to absorb as much of the heat from the sun as possible. If there was anything she did not like about flying, it was the fact that the wind drew all the heat out of her wings. If only she could manage to find a way to fly through the air without any wind to suck the heat of the sun away.

Even though her house had been built as far away as possible from the rest of the livestock she could still clearly hear them in the distance. Horses, cows, sheep, all of them could be heard by her keen ears. She could even hear the villagers as they walked through town discussing trivial matters with each other.

She opened her eyes and leapt into the air taking flight, rising into the air quickly to get high enough to not startle the nearby animals. It only took a few tight circles to gain enough altitude that she need not fear passing over the village. Below her, Arisa could see the entirety of the village even at this low altitude, such was the small size. There were only a few dozen buildings. Twenty-eight by her count.

At the center of the village was the church, or so they called it. In truth it was just the community hall. It was used more during the weeknights for celebrating and general gatherings, especially during the winter nights when it was much too cold to spend time outside. The village was too small to have a preacher so it was up to the elders to take turns in telling the villagers about a place they called hell.

Some of the elders seem to enjoy informing all the people in this village of all their deeds that will send them to this hell if they do not repent.

The dragon mused to herself as she slowly passed over the village.

I shall have to ask Ketarr about that sometime. I understand the concepts they speak of, and agree with most of what they have to say about good and evil. Even still, I have not yet grasped these ideas of heaven and hell. If one is to be sought after while the other avoided I simply do not understand why they do not just do so.

Farther outside the village were a few homesteads for the families that desired to be nearest to their farms. As she reached the edge of the village

Arisa tilted her angle and flew towards the forest where Elànde would be riding and hunting. It was ridiculous to think she would be able to see the young girl through the trees, but it always put the dragon at ease knowing that she was nearby and safe.

The girl did not have her own horse, that was simply too costly for her. But many of the villagers had given her permission to use their horses for riding lessons whenever they were not riding themselves. Many of them freely admitted that they just could not resist her earnest smile. Arisa understood her friend's position with money. She herself had no money. Even if she were to take a job and get paid she would have no way to carry the small currency often used by the humans. Instead she conducted trade with those she met.

It was easy for her to offer her services for a few weeks to any village. Most villages had need of muscle to move things or prepare new ground for seed. With her claws it was simple for her to till up the hard ground of a newly established field for the first time. This made it much easier for the humans to go back through and do final preparations with their oxen. Though she did not enjoy this as much as other jobs. It often took her many days to get the dirt completely cleaned out of her claws.

However, these jobs provided a fair trade for her to get a couple of well seasoned meals and a warm place to stay for a few nights. It is true that she had no need for cooked meals. But she and others of her kind did enjoy the new and sometimes unexpected flavors that humans could bring out of the meat with their spices. It was always a joy to her in particular to eat a meal prepared for her by the humans of Rupsê.

For Elànde, finding work was a different matter altogether. In their time at Rupsê the girl had learned many valuable skills.

She could sew to mend clothes, and had even started making pouches and other small items from scratch. Her cooking skill still left much to be desired, according to Ketarr, but she worked diligently to better herself. Cleaning, errands, watching babies, all these things and more she had learned to do with a smile on her face. Her jobs were such that they could be repeated, over and over.

For Arisa, however, staying longer than a few weeks at any village, was a different matter. She did not feel as if she was making fair trade anymore. Everything had been taken care of by her long ago. There was simply not enough work to keep even a single dragon occupied in one village. Lately she had begun to feel as if she was imposing on the village. She simply took up space and food.

No, not just lately. It has been some time. No-one has said anything to me but I cannot imagine they would be sorry to see me off to another village. Eating their food and scaring their livestock.

Arisa sighed as these things passed through her mind.

Here I am flying to try and get my problems with the child off my mind and instead I am just filling myself up with new problems. And in the end they are new problems that still involve the child.

"No, I suppose they are not really new problems. My inability to leave the child, or rather her inability to let me leave, has been at issue for some time now."

There was another problem that returned to her troubled mind once again. What had happened to the village she had found Elànde in? The loss of her own memory was closely tied to that concern. If not for the child she would have spent the last few years searching for answers. In this amount of time she could have travelled to all the villages in the area and probably found dozens of other dragons as well. Somebody must know what happened.

Arisa needed information. She was working with her own limited knowledge and had even less first-hand information. She was just not old enough nor experienced enough to unravel this mystery without help, or at the very least, without more information.

The information is out there, I just need to go find it. If I do not, something terrible like that might happen again.

She was still of the opinion that magic may have been involved in what happened. After so many years without regaining her memory it did not seem likely her amnesia was simply due to some head injury caused by crashing into a building. A couple hundred humans don't just vanish without a trace. Nor does a village burn itself to the ground without any bodies remaining behind.

It was just too strange. No, magic had to be involved somehow. And if magic had been once again awakened in this world then that was something that all dragons must be made aware of. The last war brought about by magic had cost the lives of many dragons, and tens of thousands of humans. The loss of life was great, but the dragons had fought back immediately before magic could spread to the rest of the world.

Arisa checked the position of the sun. It had been some time since she had left the village. The day was growing to a close and Elànde would likely be returning from hunting at any moment. The child would be upset with her for being gone and not telling her. Having had no particular destination in mind she was still near the village. She had simply been making large, lazy circles through the air.

As she approached the village once more she spotted Ketarr in one of the fields below. He seemed to be inspecting the wheat that was beginning to grow. She still wanted to talk to him about this ridiculous idea of Elànde flying with her. And it would be a good chance to discuss some of the other things that had been on her mind of late as well.

It is unlikely Elànde will interrupt our conversation. She should not return from riding for a short while still.

Arisa glided down through the air to land beside the field and waited for Ketarr. He had seen her descent and was already making his way over to her. Once he arrived and they had made their greetings she impatiently told him of what was on her mind.

She had meant to primarily discuss that absurd flying idea. Instead Arisa found herself unleashing her fears about her having stayed too long and her inability to travel abroad and solve this mystery that plagued her. Ketarr just listened silently as he always did. He was a good listener, he knew when to be quiet and when to interject.

The fact that he had been silent through her whole tirade disturbed her. It usually meant he had found something wrong with her logic and would set her straight momentarily.

"That has all been on your mind for some time?"

"Yes. It has. I did not want to speak of it before. Actually, I had no intention of speaking of it even now. You usually stop me before I get this far."

"I thought it best to let you speak your mind this time."

Ketarr smiled in his soft, encouraging manner. The same one which he always gave her whenever he was about to correct her on some point that she should have realized herself.

"Hmph."

"I believe you are entirely correct."

"What? What do you mean? Correct about what?"

"Everything, or near enough."

"Then... the villagers do resent my presence?"

"No, no. I assure you we do not resent you in

any way. But you are correct that it is no longer a fair trade. You do your best to provide for yourself, but even still you consume much of our food and our time while we prepare it for you. The animals are indeed uneasy in your presence, though that was dealt with as best we could early on by moving you outside the village."

Shocked by his abrupt confirmation of her fears Arisa just stared back and allowed her shoulders to droop. The old man, however, continued on in a softer tone.

"Early on we had much work that you could do for us, but over the last year or two there just has not been much that you could do. With your help, everything has been repaired that needed to be. You have expanded our fields for us to the point that we could not manage anything larger. So, recently there has just been very little you could do for us. Which means, that what we provide you is the greater to what you provide for us.

"Elànde has tried her best as well, but she also fails to provide a fair trade with us. Oh she does help out from time to time with things that would be difficult for us grownups to do ourselves. Certainly she is nearly always successful when hunting. But in the end, all the sewing, cooking and everything else she does, we could do ourselves without her help. While she does all these things she is consuming our food, our beds, and our time."

"I do not understand. Why then do you let us stay? If it would be better for you to send us away why have you not done so? I thought at the very least Elànde was providing fair trade by doing things for everyone."

"Babies and young children are similar are they not? They eat our food and sleep in our beds and consume our time taking care of them. If we give them a task to perform could we not do the same task in a fraction of the time? Why then would we keep them around instead of sending them away?"

"Yes, I suppose that is true. But they are your kin. Do not humans put greater importance on other humans when they are kindred?"

Ketarr smiled broadly.

"That is true, but do you really think I could spend nearly one quarter of my life in *unfair* trade with my own children if it were just kinship that kept me from giving up on them? Life is not about *fair trade*. That is a concept for business, not for everyday life."

"I still do not understand. If it is never fair, why would you continue to let us stay?"

"Because my wise friend, we are not trading with you. We are investing in our friendship with both of you. The same as our own children, we invest in them for the future. If I spend time raising my own children, then when I am old they may spend time helping me at the times I am too frail. I provide time and resources to the two of you because I believe you will one day do something in return. If not for us, then for others in a different village.

"Do not misunderstand me though. I do not

say that I *expect* something in return. I simply *believe* that you will provide something, even if it is not for me. Tell me, the dragons keep good relations with humans, yes?"

"Of course."

"How many villages have you visited more than once?"

"I do not know for sure. Perhaps three?"

"And how many villages have you visited in all your travels?"

"Well over a forty."

"Then why do you bother to keep good relations with those you are likely never to see again? Why would it be trouble for you if you caused harm to a village by making a feast out of their livestock if you never went back again?"

"It would cause trouble for the next dragon to visit that village. They would not be made welcome. It is also possible it would cause trouble for me at another village if they heard what I had done. If that were to happen I would lose out on the chance to learn from that new village."

Ketarr nodded slowly as he responded.

"Indeed, that is a very likely outcome. So you keep good relations with humans so that it will benefit you later, as well as benefit others of your kind. You are *investing* in the future, are you not?"

Unsure exactly what he was getting at Arisa gave her reply slowly.

"I suppose."

"We humans do the same. We *invest* in the

future. Oh we may go about it differently than you dragons do. But when it comes down to it, we are no different. Whether it be you or another dragon, we provide food and a place to stay because we hope that you, or another of your kind, will help us in our time of need. If a nearby village met with disaster due to a flood and had to rebuild many of their homes, would you go help?"

"Of course. With my help they would be able to fell trees and rebuild much quicker than if they were to attempt it by themselves."

"And would you expect *fair trade* in return before you left? Would you demand from them that they feed you an appropriate amount of well-seasoned food before departing? Or would you instead take one good meal and leave?"

"Hrm."

Arisa thought hard before she answered. She could tell that she was trapped and would not be able to escape the outcome of this conversation. It was better to admit defeat with some pride. Because the truth was, Ketarr was entirely correct.

"I suppose… I would take one meal and ask them to be friendly towards the next dragon that visited their village. I will grant you that. But it still does not sit well with me for you to provide so much to me without being able to repay you."

"There are ways for you to repay us. I have not brought them up before because I did not think you would easily accept it. You want to repay the kindness that we have shown to you and Elànde.

You also desire to expand your knowledge about what happened back in Konsau, which you are unable to do by staying here. What I have in mind may solve both of your problems as well as a few of ours."

The dragon was wary of this old man. He had a twinkle in his eye that she did not like.

"How so?"

"It would involve letting that girl fly with you."

Arisa sighed.

"I believe I have already lost to you in the discussion of fair trade. I do not wish to begin another just to lose again. So for the moment I will accept that as a possibility and hear you out. But I reserve the right to decline at any time."

"That is to be expected, and quite fair. What I have in mind is letters."

"Huh?"

"I am suggesting that you and Elànde can begin to make deliveries between the various villages in this area."

"What do you mean, *deliveries*?"

"What I mean, is that you and Elànde could start delivering letters while you fly between the villages gathering information. I have friends whom I only get to see once every few years, if even that often. Having the chance to send and receive letters with those acquaintances on a regular basis would mean a lot to many of us."

"How would doing such a simple task allow

us to repay the years of kindness you have shown us? There is no way that could balance the debt we owe you."

"It always makes me happy when I get the chance to explain something simple to you."

Arisa grumbled out her reply.

"That seems to happen far too frequently of late for my liking."

"It is simply because I have a different way of looking at things than do you. As to the balance, how long do we humans live?"

"I believe that to be between sixty and seventy years?"

"That is a fairly accurate estimate. If I only get to visit with my friends once every few years, then that does not provide me with many opportunities to talk to them. Getting a chance to send and receive letters every few weeks would multiply those opportunities tenfold. That, my dear, is very much worth the time and energy we have spent raising that young girl these past years."

"And what about me?"

"Yes, it would indeed make everything we have done for you worth it as well."

Arisa sighed and looked to the sky for a minute before returning her attention to Ketarr.

"Have you already discussed all of this with Elànde?"

"I have. In fact it was she who discussed it to me. Shortly after your arrival in Rupsê I had made the suggestion of the harness to allow her to fly with you, once the both of you were ready. But recently it was her idea to give something back to the village."

"Her idea? Why would she come up with an idea such as this?"

"I believe she had the same concerns you do. She wanted to do something for the village as thanks. So Elànde came up with the entire idea of delivering letters all on her own. She even drew up some modifications for the harness that would allow the two of you to carry the letters and even some small packages."

"So what should I do?"

"That is something you must decide for yourself, of course. But, if your pride is the only thing preventing you from saying yes, then I believe you will have to make a decision. Is your pride in fair trade more powerful than your personal pride of not allowing the girl to fly with you?"

* * * * *

Arisa had taken flight and was heading to the other side of the village where Elànde would be returning. Her talk with Ketarr did not exactly make her feel better, but it did give her a clear understanding of the position she was in. That was something the old man seemed to excel in.

She knew he was right about one thing. She had been making excuses to herself for not allowing Elànde to fly with her. Even through the various excuses she offered, Ketarr and Marika had quietly listened and calmly refuted them with valid facts. It came down to her pride. She did not want the girl to fly with her because she was afraid to be seen with her. It would hurt her pride to have other dragons scoff at her for allowing such a thing.

What she had to decide was, did she really care if others looked down upon her? What is it exactly they would look down on her for? Would she herself look down on another dragon if she saw that dragon flying with a human rider? These were all things that had been bothering her. Things that she needed to decide for herself.

On the other side of the field coming up before her, Arisa could see Elànde taking the saddle off the horse she had been riding. On the ground beside her was a small fox that she had managed to bring down with her bow. As usual the girl worked diligently to make sure the horse was properly cared for and everything put back in its proper place.

"Elànde!"

The girl looked up at the circling dragon and waved excitedly.

"When you are finished, come to the field."

Elànde waved once more in acknowledgement and returned to the horse. She had learned well how to care for the animals of the village. The other children her age only wished to do the enjoyable parts. They wanted to ride without putting in the effort of preparing the horse for riding or rubbing the horse down afterwards. Elànde had taken to the entire job. She seemed to enjoy doing the job from beginning to end, and doing it all herself.

Descending upon the field, Arisa landed softly and waited for her friend to arrive. She still didn't know what she wanted to do herself, but Arisa had decided it was something the two of them should decide together. After all this time, it would not be fair to the child to make a decision that affected the both of them without at least consulting her on the matter.

After a few minutes Elànde came running across the field. She was smiling broadly.

I suppose that is to be expected. She is normally the one that comes to me to talk rather than me telling her I want to talk.

"How was your riding, child?"

"It was good. Merik is so much fun to ride. She does really good with jumping."

Arisa understood why humans would name their animals. It made it easy to identify them during conversation. It intrigued her, however, that they always seemed to refer to them with so much love. As if they were a part of the family, or at the very least close friends.

"I see. That is good. I am very glad."

The girl, still smiling, looked up at the dragon. It was obvious she wanted to ask what her friend wanted to talk to her about but she was being very patient.

"You still wish to fly with me?"

Elànde's eyes grew wide in surprise. She nodded quickly.

"Yes, very much!"

"Even though it may not be safe for you to do so?"

"The harness Marika has made will keep me safe."

"I do trust her and Ketarr, but even still. There is a chance something may go wrong. The harness may break, or… or something."

The girl's surprise quickly changed to concern at Arisa's sudden change of mood. It was not like her to be unsure of her words when speaking.

"Arisa, what's wrong?"

"In truth, it is not your safety I am truly worried about. I trust in the harness Marika has made."

"Then what is it?"

Arisa looked away from the girl momentarily. Looking up at the sky she sighed inwardly, knowing she had put this off long enough. There was no denying the truth, the selfish truth, behind her reasons for not wanting Elànde to fly with her.

"It shames me to admit it. But I am worried about what others would think if they saw us flying together. I do not know how I would respond to such a situation and that has left me uneasy."

"You mean if other dragons saw us?"

"… Yes. I have told you before of the pride dragons have. While flying with a human riding upon me does not directly hurt my pride, at least not anymore, it is something that is just not done.

Because of this, I cannot know what others will think of me. I cannot even say what I would think if I were to see another dragon being ridden by a human."

Elànde stepped close to her friend's drooping head and pressed her own forehead against the dragon's cheek.

"I never wanted to make you uncomfortable. If, you do not wish to fly with me, I will stop asking."

"In truth I do not know. I have not made up my mind. That is why I wish to know your feelings on the matter. I know you wish to fly with me, but *why* do you wish to fly with me?"

"Well… It's not the first time I have thought about that question. Marika and I have discussed it at length many times."

Arisa watched as the young girl stepped back and looked into her eye. Elànde was quiet for a moment before continuing to answer her question.

"I know that things may go wrong. As you said yourself, the harness may break. We could get caught in a storm and I might get sick from flying through it. If things go badly enough, I might even die. Even still, I want to fly with you. I want to always be with you no matter what. You're my friend, and my family."

"If we are both made to be outcasts by our fellow kin by traveling together?"

"Then I shall gladly become an outcast with you. But I don't think that will happen to us. I can't imagine anybody from Rupsê would make either of us an outcast, and I think you know that too. As for your kin, we would just have to see what they say."

Arisa quietly watched the child before her. She was thinking upon those words. It was true that she was bringing up the worst possible result. A much more mild reaction from other dragons was far more likely. Still, she could not help but dwell on that outcome.

"I suppose you are right. The humans here would not think anything bad of either of us if we were to travel together. As for my fellow dragons... if you are willing to share in the danger of flying with me then we will just have to wait and see what they say."

Arisa smiled a little nervously as the child's face brightened.

"So, it's alright if I fly with you?"

"I cannot say whether or not it is fine, but we will give it a try and see how things go."

"Thank you! Thank you! I'm so excited. I can't wait to tell Marika and Ketarr that you said yes."

"Yes well, while I am certain they can hear you from where we are in this field, I am sure they would rather have you tell them in person. Let us—"

Arisa stopped mid-sentence and looked up towards the northern sky. Elànde followed her friends gaze but could see nothing.

"Arisa? What is it? What are you looking at?"

"I heard..."

Elànde stepped back as her friend lifted her

head and roared into the sky. It was loud, too loud. She could hear all the animals in the village complaining in fear at the sound. Her own head ached and reverberated with the overload to her hearing.

"What's going on?"

"A dragon is coming. There was a call looking for any other dragons to respond. Whomever they are, they shall be here shortly."

"Another dragon? Why?"

Arisa looked down at her with a strange expression. It wasn't quite a smile. There was something more to it. Something she rarely showed. A hint, just a small hint, that she was being playful.

"Child, have I gone somewhere and returned in the past three minutes that I was not aware of? I have been here with you. I do not know why a dragon approaches, but it seems to be an important matter. It is not our way for dragons to fly around roaring for attention. There must be some reason. There, they come, do you see them?"

After squinting her eyes she finally saw a small speck approaching. It looked like a tiny sparrow, but it was growing. Growing rapidly.

"They're so fast. Is that really a dragon?"

"Yes. When dragons push themselves to the limit, we can move at incredible speeds. But it is not sustainable. For them to be traveling so quickly…"

* * * * *

Arisa never finish her thought, at-least not out loud. Elànde could make out the color of the dragon already as it approached. The wings and most of the body seemed to be green. No, not green. Turquoise. The dragon was turquoise she was sure of it now. Indeed, she could not mistake it with how close it had come. Already the dragon was descending to land.

"Stay close to me child."

There was no time for Elànde to respond. The dragon was approaching so quickly that she feared it might crash into them. With a mighty gust of wind the dragon winged backwards a few times and then alighted onto the ground amidst a cloud of dust.

"Greetings. I am Arisa, daughter of Tirza."

"And to you, I am Wuldaq, son of Bünor."

Arisa bowed her head in greeting and turned her attention to the awestruck girl beside her.

"This is Elànde, daughter of Marlene."

Feeling a slight nudge from her friend she looked up at the dragon beside her.

"Do not stare at him, child, it is impolite."

"O-oh, I'm sorry. It is a pleasure to meet you!"

She made an awkward bow of her head, trying to imitate the greeting he gave to her.

"I serve as messenger to bring word to all dragons of this land. There is to be a meeting of all dragons in six days' time. It's to begin at first light. All dragons who are not feral are to attend without exception."

"Where is this meeting to take place?"

"There is a large mountain two days' flight to the south-east of here. Half a day's flight due east from there will bring you to a plateau. The meeting will be held there."

"Two and a half days' travel. That does not leave much time. What is this about?"

As Wuldaq glanced at her, Elànde could feel his hesitation. Pressing herself against her friend she waited for him to continue.

"Over the past three moons there have been reports from numerous dragons. During their travels they have come across many villages that have been burned to the ground. The villagers were... "

Elànde covered her mouth and looked up at her friend. Her's was not the only village destroyed. This had happened to others. It was Arisa who responded for the both of them by finishing his statement.

"All missing. No sign of bodies and no evidence that they left the village prior to its burning."

"Yes. You have heard of this before then."

"No. But I, that is we, experienced it for ourselves."

Both dragons looked at the child standing next to them. The tears on her cheeks were obvious despite her attempts to look brave. Arisa lowered her head and touched Elànde's forehead before continuing.

"This girl is from a nearby village that met

with the same fate. I cannot say how, but I was somehow involved in what happened. Four years ago she found me in one of the burning buildings, unconscious. Everyone but her had already vanished. When she herself awoke her parents and all the others were gone. I myself have no memory of how I arrived in such a condition."

"This is the first time I have heard that anyone survived whatever has been happening. If it was so long ago then your village may well have been the first. You have my apologies little one, I'm very sorry for your loss. To my understanding, your village makes the fifteenth village to be razed, though all the others have been found recently."

"What of other lands?"

"There have been unconfirmed reports that the same thing is happening elsewhere. A number of dragons have been sent to determine if indeed the same thing is happening in the nearby regions. My younger sister was sent to the west to scout. She is supposed to return in time for the council."

"I understand."

The smaller dragon looked down at Elànde again. It was not really fair to call him *small*. Compared to herself he was still huge. But he appeared to be smaller while standing next to Arisa.

"I wish I had found you before now. I don't intend to bring sorrow to your heart by reminding you of the past, but to our knowledge you are the only human who has survived. If there was time for you to travel to the plateau as well, any information would be useful. As it is we shall have to rely on what you have shared with Arisa."

"No, she will join us."

"What?"

"Huh?"

Elànde looked at her friend only to see her looking back upon her expectantly. She recovered only slightly from her surprise before responding to Arisa's waiting stare.

"You mean, I should come?"

"If you are willing. As Wuldaq has said, any information could be valuable. Even though you have told me all you remember, we cannot discount the possibility that something new will come to your memory by hearing the accounts of others. I do not want to cause you pain if it is too difficult to remember such things.

"Before you give your answer, however, you must know that there are suspicions I have had since our first meeting about what might have happened. I have never told you of these before now. I would not normally mention them without proof or evidence of some kind, but I believe at this meeting all must be shared. You yourself may be able to shed additional light on my suspicions, but it may bring up very painful memories."

"How could she arrive in time? It would take far too long for a human to travel to the plateau."

Arisa ignored her kin's question and continued to look to Elànde for an answer.

"You will be with me the whole time?"

"I shall."

Elànde looked back towards the village for the first time since Wuldaq's arrival. Everyone had heard Arisa's roar and a crowd had formed at the edge of the field. Nearly the entire village was there watching.

She could see Ketarr and Marika standing in front watching her. They may not have known exactly what was going on, but even at their distance it would have been difficult to not hear most of what the dragons had said. Both of them gave her an encouraging nod.

"I'll go with you."

Arisa nodded with finality and turned back to Wuldaq. Elànde had spent years with Arisa, but she still found it difficult sometimes to read expressions on the dragon's face. But it was clear, even to her, that confusion reigned in Wuldaq's emotions now.

"She will fly with me. We shall both arrive in time for the meeting in six days' time."

Wuldaq looked back and forth between the pair before him. After a moment's time to fully comprehend what had been said he gave them a somewhat mischievous smile before replying.

"I'll look forward to your arrival. This should prove to be a very interesting sight."

CHAPTER 6

"How does it sit? Is it causing you any discomfort?"

"I do not believe so…"

Arisa wiggled around in the harness to make sure she still had full mobility without interference from it. Marika and some of the other ladies had spent the last two days and nights working fervently to finish the harness in time for their departure. There was little time to lose if they were to make the plateau by the appointed time. By her estimate it would take them four days' travel. She knew that she herself was not accustomed to long distance travel any more and would likely become winded easily.

Still skeptical, Wuldaq had left shortly after Arisa's declaration that they would both be in attendance. After relaying his news to the rest of the village Arisa and Elànde informed them of their intention to travel together to this meeting. She expected them to be more difficult, considering they had not even finished the harness let alone tested it.

Instead Arisa had been shocked by their response. Ketarr simply nodded and asked if they were likely to return soon. She had hesitated, since she had not even spoke to Elànde of this yet, but responded that there was a good chance they would not return for many cycles of the moon. With that, he turned to the rest of the village and declared that the following evening would be a feast for their friends, but until then there was much to do to prepare for their departure.

The feast had been last night and they had all eaten their fill, especially Arisa and Elànde. They decided that it might be some time before they got to eat like that again, so they didn't hold back. Just a few minutes ago while they were fastening the harness Arisa had wished she had held back just a little bit and not eaten so much. Not that she would say anything out loud.

"It fits very well. It is well made Marika."

Some distance away, Elànde stood quietly next to Ketarr. The girl was fidgeting nervously while Marika talked to Arisa about the harness. Worry filled her mind that the harness wouldn't work. If that happened, she knew that she would have to give leave to Arisa to go alone. From what she had said last night it might be many moons before she would return.

"Do not fret so much. It will be fine."

Elànde looked up to see Ketarr smiling down on her with his usual reassuring smile. They had made many small modifications to the harness the previous day in preparation for their journey. Originally, Marika had designed it with only short flights between villages in mind. There had been only one small pouch, just big enough to contain enough provisions for one or two nights. Now there were enough pouches to contain provisions for many nights. By Elànde's estimates she could easily survive two weeks before she needed to restock on supplies.

"I am worried for Arisa as much as I am the harness. This is all so sudden. She had been concerned about what a single dragon might say to her after seeing us flying together. Now we are getting ready to go see many dragons all at once."

"I am sure she considered that before she committed herself to the task. Do not fret over things you can do nothing about. She has been worrying over these things for the past week. But look at her now. I have not seen her look this pleased in a long time. In fact, I don't think the timing could have been better for this meeting."

"What do you mean?"

"She will be facing all her fears at once. If she can survive being in such a large gathering of her fellow dragons with you riding on her back, then she will never have to worry about what others will say again. I believe she is aware of that fact too. It may even be what gives her the strength to do this so suddenly."

"Hmm."

Elànde and Ketarr looked back at the dragon as she gave one massive shake all over in a final attempt to dislodge the harness.

"Please do stand back Marika. I wish to test my wings now."

"Go ahead my dear. I'm not so frail that you will knock me over."

Arisa bowed her head to the old lady and

then stood tall. As she flapped her wings she pushed off the ground with her forelegs and stood on her haunches, using the power of her wings to keep balance.

A small noise next to him brought Ketarr's attention away from the dragon to the girl still standing near him.

"What is it that makes you giggle?"

"Her. She looks like a dog begging for a treat. Don't you think so too?"

"Ha! I suppose you are right. Though I daresay you should be careful to never say that loud enough for her to hear."

"Yes, I suppose you are right."

Arisa came back down to all fours softer than Elànde ever thought would be possible. She raised her wing and addressed old lady again.

"Marika, could you tighten the rear-left cinch a bit? Just a little more. Yes, that should do it."

Elànde watched as Marika ducked out of the way again before Arisa lowered her wing. The harness had seven buckles that could be adjusted. One on each side of the strap running underneath her belly and behind her wings. A similar strap with buckles was fastened around her belly but in front of her wings.

This kept her wings free of all the straps so there was no danger of getting tangled up. It also had the eerie effect of making it look as though the two belly straps did not exist as her wings folded up neatly over the top of the straps, hiding them completely. Another strap ran in front around her chest, also with a buckle on each side. A final strap with the last buckle ran underneath from the chest strap back to the middle strap.

"Very well. I suppose I should make my test flight before we leave. I shall be back shortly."

With that, Arisa took flight for real. She made a few small circles with short beats of her wings before venturing away from the field they were in. Elànde looked in amazement at her friend. The entire harness nearly disappeared from sight as soon as she was in the air.

Marika had taken great care with the harness. The entire apparatus had been made with soft deerskin underneath the leather. The straps had deerskin on the exposed side as well, but this had been dyed violet to match Arisa's scales. The buckles themselves had an extra flap of leather and fur to keep them concealed once they had been fastened. From even a short distance away it was nearly impossible to tell that she actually had anything but the saddle atop her back.

Even Elànde hated calling it a saddle, but it could be described as nothing else. It had additional straps that Elànde would use to secure herself with. Once in place these straps went over her legs so that it would be nearly impossible for her to fall off. On each side there were three straps for the rider. One was just above the ankle, another just below the knee and the final went over the thigh. Additionally, there were handholds sewn into the top of the saddle for her to hold on to.

There was little more than a narrow strip of leather to the saddle itself, but with all the pouches for carrying supplies it looked much larger. Each pouch could be removed and carried separately. Or, when they became empty, they could be rolled up and stored together. As it was now, each pouch had been loaded to the fullest with various supplies. Elànde had been given food, water, and blankets in addition to her change of clothes.

The amount of supplies she was taking reminded her that it may very well be some time before they return. With a tear forming in her eye she looked up to the sky once more to watch her friend. Arisa had travelled some distance away and was now turning to return to the field when Elànde finally caught sight of her again.

The speed with which Arisa was returning astonished Elànde. She had thought that Wuldaq might have been an extraordinarily fast dragon. It would make sense for a fast dragon to be chosen as messenger for the other dragons. Arisa now rivaled the speed they had seen from Wuldaq the day before. In a moment she was upon them and performed the same landing by changing her angle to almost standing in midair and using her wings to halt her momentum.

After a short blast of air from Arisa's wings to those standing on the ground she alighted a few dozen paces away. As she approached them Arisa addressed Marika.

"It could not have been designed better. You have done an excellent job. If it will serve Elànde as well as it does me then I can see no reason why either of us should have any trouble."

"I am pleased to hear that, my dear. I believe the two of you will have to make daily adjustments to the buckles until everything has finished stretching. Once that is done it should be a simple matter to put it back on each morning. Though I think you may have to use every muscle you have to lift it."

This last bit was directed at Elànde who had arrived next to them. It's true she was not entirely sure how she would manage to remove the harness each night, let alone replace it in the mornings. They had made it as light as possible, but there was still a lot of material. The two of them would just have to manage somehow in the end.

"Uh, you won't be flying that fast with me will you?"

Arisa made a noise that was somewhere between a snort and a chuckle. It was rare for any of them to see the dragon give any indication of humor. Elànde took this as a hearty laugh and smiled as the dragon responded to her.

"Do not worry, little one. I do not travel at that speed very often. I just wanted to be sure that I could still exert my full energy even with the harness. Now then, I suppose it is time for us to go. It may take only two and a half days for a dragon to make the flight, but I can fly much further than I suspect you will be ready for. As it is we shall have to be diligent to see that we arrive in time."

"I guess, it is time for us to leave then."

Most of the crying and goodbyes had been said last night during the feast, but that did not mean there was not room for fresh tears now. Elànde hugged Marika and Ketarr once more before climbing up onto Arisa.

"We'll be back someday, I promise!"

"Of course you will child. We look forward to seeing you again. Both of you."

Arisa bowed her head deeply to each of them in turn.

"Thank you for everything you have done for the two of us. We should have perished long ago if not for the kindness you and your village have shown to us."

"Safe travels to you."

"Are you strapped in, Elànde?"

The girl felt so very small. She had been up on Arisa's back many times, but this time felt different. This time she knew they were going to fly. Reaching over she touched her mother's bracelet with her right hand. It always gave her courage to feel the strength of its metal against her fingertips.

"Yes, I am ready."

"Alright. Let us go then."

Arisa turned to face south and stretched her wings out. The sun felt so very good as it always did, but this time there was something more. She felt even warmer than she normally would. Yes, having a friend along would make this trip much more enjoyable. She crouched low and called back one last time to her friend before leaping into the air.

"You had best not become sick to your stomach up there or I shall never forgive you!"

* * * * *

It had only been an hour and Elànde's muscles were already sore and fatigued. Her hands had blisters and her legs were aching something terrible. She felt as if she had been riding a horse for an entire day without rest. Because of the wind she was well aware that they were traveling quite fast, but looking down at the ground far below it felt as if they were barely moving at all.

When first they had taken flight Arisa had been careful to fly as slow as possible. Over the past hour she had been steadily increasing their speed as her new rider became accustomed to the wind and sensations of flight.

"How are you doing up there, Elànde?"

The wind against her ears made the girl feel like she had to shout back to be heard. It was incredibly loud. Never when riding a horse had she ever come close to experiencing this much wind rushing against her.

"I'm fine, I think!"

"I can hear you just fine, so you do not need to strain your voice. With a little practice you will not even notice the wind anymore, it will be as if we were holding a conversation while standing on the ground. Give it time and you will eventually be accustomed to it."

"How long will we be traveling today? I'm sorry but I am already so very tired of holding on."

"Then do not hold on. The harness was designed so that you need not use your own strength to stay on. That is what the straps are for. Allow yourself to relax and just use your hands to keep balance."

Elànde relaxed her grip but instinctively tightened her legs against the dragon. There were multiple straps holding her safe and secure, but even still she felt that she would fall if she were to let go.

"No, no. You must relax child! Do not tighten your legs. The straps will hold secure. By trying to hold on yourself you are just fighting against them. Allow the straps to do most of the work, focus your energies instead on fighting against the wind so that you do not blow backwards."

It was not a very comforting thought. Being blown backwards atop the dragon would likely prove very painful with the lower half of her body fastened in place. Elànde grimaced at the idea. She knew in her mind that she was safe and would not fall, but transferring that knowledge to the rest of her body was proving more difficult than she expected.

"Now, to answer your question, we shall fly until you can fly no longer. I expect you will give out long before I tire. I imagine it will take us slightly longer than expected so we shall probably arrive a little late. As such I would like to fly as long as you are able to stand, or rather I suppose, to sit."

"If we are able to take rests occasionally I think I can manage for as long as you like. But I shan't be pleasant company when this is over!"

A hearty chortle rippled through the dragon beneath her.

"When this is over, we shall both rest. Look there ahead of us, do you see that river?"

Elànde squinted her eyes while looking forward. She could see what looked like a small trickle of a stream, but no river.

"I see a stream, nothing more. Is that what you mean?"

"Yes, it is a river. A rather wide one in fact. You shall see as we draw closer to it. Do you remember when we first met, you asked me why you must be so watchful of your surroundings and I told you how a river could be dangerous even from the air. This shall be your first lesson in flying."

With that the dragon shifted her wings and began a swift descent towards the ground. Elànde could already see that the stream was indeed larger than she had first thought. Below her the distance to the ground was decreasing steadily and she could already make out details below. The girl had also become aware that she had fiercely tightened her grip on the dragon.

In short order they had dropped to the height of the tallest trees and there Arisa leveled off. Another shift of her wings and she was back-beating slightly causing them to slow down. Once they were to the speed a crow might fly she once again changed the angle of her wings and began gliding, with only an occasional beat.

"This is as slow as I can safely fly. The river ahead is quite wide and will provide a good lesson for you at this altitude. When we cross over it I shall do my best to not compensate for the change in the air currents. I will keep us out of danger but I want you to feel the effects of the water on the air."

The girl nodded but did not respond, except for another increase in the pressure of her legs upon the dragon beneath her.

"And relax your legs!"

She winced at the reprimand. It wasn't as if she thought Arisa was angry at her. Elànde wanted to prove that she could be a good rider. She knew very well what she should be doing already, but getting her own body to comply and stay relaxed was proving more difficult than the girl had expected.

As they approached the river she looked down at the ground below and was amazed at how fast everything was passing by. Arisa had said this was the slowest she could fly and even still it seemed like they were making great speed. Watching from the ground it had never occurred to her that her friend was actually moving so quickly.

Approaching the edge of the river she could already feel the air change. It was cooler than it was a moment ago. At the same time she also noticed the ride was becoming rougher. It wasn't much, but instead of a smooth gliding motion Arisa had begun to gently rock back and forth.

"You are swaying, is that because of the river?"

"Yes. The air is not consistent here."

Arisa suddenly tilted to the left, as if to emphasize her point, before quickly flapping her wings twice to right herself. Looking down at her hands Elànde could see that they had gone white from how tightly she was gripping the saddle. The rocking continued as they glided across the river. Near the far edge one more sudden change in the air currents caused the pair to rise quickly before suddenly dropping back to their previous height.

They had gotten a late start and it was already approaching lunch time. Up to now Elànde had been idly thinking about food. Their last sudden altitude shift caused Elànde to became distinctly aware that she no longer had a desire to eat.

"How do you fare up there? We shall rest here for a few minutes."

Her friend had begun flapping her wings again and was slowly turning back toward the river and dropping towards the ground.

"I don't... feel so good."

"Hmph. Wait until we land before you purge your stomach. I am not currently in the mood to take a bath."

A few moments later and they were on solid ground. One of them was at any rate. Elànde began to slowly unfasten all the straps holding her in with unsteady hands. Once free she managed to crawl down, somewhat more gracefully than expected, before collapsing upon the ground. Her legs were too wobbly to support her own weight just yet.

"We have only been flying a short time, child. At this rate I am not sure we shall be able to make it to the gathering in time if you cannot managed to fly even this long."

"N-no, I can manage. I promise I will not make you be late. I just need a minute to stretch my legs."

Arisa watched Elànde begin walking, somewhat shakily, to the river.

"Are you sure you are fine child? You look a bit pale."

The girl didn't respond right away, but did manage to cross the short distance to the river. After splashing water on her face and taking a few drinks she looked back to Arisa.

"Is it always that rough when you fly over water?"

"Only when flying so low. When I fly higher the changes in the air currents are more subtle. However if I am flying as low as we were, such as if I am hunting, then it is usually much worse. The faster I am moving when passing through those air currents the more pronounced the effect."

"But wouldn't getting through it all quickly be better?"

"Better for me perhaps, but I think not for you until you are accustomed to flying. It took us nearly ten seconds to cross this river. In that time you felt the changes to my flying did you not?"

"Yes. You had been flying very gently. But when we were over the river you were rocking back and forth and, umm, lurching a bit."

Arisa could not fault the child for telling the truth about her flying. Even so she did not really appreciate the bluntness of such a statement.

"I have not flown that poorly since I was a hatchling. It took great concentration to not immediately correct for all the changes in the air. I have done so for so long it comes to me as easily as walking does to you. You were not much help yourself, shifting your weight this way and that way. You do not weigh much, but even the smallest change can make me tilt to one side or the other while flying."

Pausing momentarily, Arisa took a few drinks from the cold river before continuing.

"However, with all those changes affecting my flying over a ten second span of time, how much more pronounced would it be if I were flying faster and the changes all happened at the same time?"

"Oh. I guess you would have to correct for all of them at once, right?"

"Indeed. It is also a simple matter for me and comes naturally, but if I am distracted and not giving proper attention to what else is around me, well then, something unsightly might happen."

Elànde mused over that a moment.

"I suppose that is true. You might even hit a

tree if your course was changed while fighting the river."

"That has not happened for some time!"

"Huh?"

"I have not hit... That is to say, it was only when I was a hatchling and still learning to fly that I ever came close to hitting something."

"Did you?"

Arisa gave a rather unfriendly look to the child looking up at her.

"Yes. A few times I have flown into trees while learning the finer points of flight."

The girl giggled slightly and then burst out in laughter.

"It is not funny child. And it hurt a great deal as well."

"I'm sorry. I didn't mean to laugh. I just can't imagine you ever flying into something. Whenever I watch you fly you are always so graceful."

"Well remember that grace takes practice. If you wish to be as graceful as I am in flight then it shall take much practice on your part as well. Speaking of practice, we should resume our journey."

Standing up, Elànde leaned against the dragon for a moment. Her legs were still unsteady, but not nearly as unsteady as when she had first dismounted a few minutes ago. It was going to be a long trip. Looking back the way they had come, it felt so very strange. They had only been flying for a little over an hour and already everything that was familiar was gone. Even this river they stood at was unknown to her.

"Do you wish to go back?"

She looked up at the questioning eyes before returning her gaze towards what was behind them. That which was a known and safe place to her. Shaking her head Elànde turned around and faced the unknown. Everything before her was strange. Mountains that had once been obscured by trees and hills now stood tall before her. Even the smells somehow seemed different.

"No. I want to go on. Maybe what is back there is safer for me. Ketarr and Marika were so very nice to me, to both of us. But you are the only family I have."

With that she climbed up the harness and settled into the saddle.

"You're the only family I think I shall ever have. I wish to stay with you forever."

"Forever is a very long time. We do not know what the future may hold for either of us. There may come a time when we must part ways."

Elànde reached down and began fastening the straps around her legs. As she straightened up a strange smile came to her face when she looked in the direction they were heading.

"Then I shall stay with you for as long as I am able. And I dare anyone, including you, to try and separate us!"

"Child, you are hopeless."

"Maybe I am hopeless, but what of you? Do

you plan to leave me at the next village or shall we travel together as family?"

"Hah. I believe then, that I am equally as hopeless. Now let us continue this journey."

CHAPTER 7

"I'm sorry that I am making you late."

Arisa could tell her companion was sad without even having to look at her. The small quiet voice told her all she needed to know about the emotional state of her friend.

Now near the end of their journey's second day they were not as far along as the dragon would have hoped. The child had done admirably but was simply unable to endure flying for long periods of time. By necessity they had been forced to make numerous stops throughout both days.

"It is nothing to worry about, child. We shall be late, but not overly so. The assembly is to begin at first light the day after tomorrow. I suspect we shall reach the mountain Wuldaq spoke of shortly before sundown tomorrow. If we can manage to fly into the night a little each day then I believe we can arrive shortly after the assembly begins."

Clenching her fists, Elànde felt responsible for slowing down her friend. It was supposed to be a two and half day journey but would take them more than four days. This was not how she wanted to travel with Arisa. She did not wish to cause her trouble.

"We can fly faster, or later into the night if we need to. I don't want you to be late."

"As I said, do not let it concern you. I know

you are tired so we shall only travel a little farther tonight before stopping. Wuldaq will be able to relay enough of our situation that some tardiness will not be unexpected. The speaker of the assembly shall know we are coming."

As she was talking a warm air current caught her wings. Stretching herself she spread out her wings as far as she could and allowed the air to lift them even higher into the air while she rested. Allowing herself to glide through the warm air Arisa was able to shift her attention fully to the girl.

Elànde's hands squeezed hard upon the harness. Her legs quivered lightly against Arisa's sides. It was obvious the girl was nearing her limit for the day. She had hoped they might arrive the night before the assembly. However, it was obvious she was pushing the girl too hard as it was. Arisa was accustomed to flying for long periods of time without rest. Elànde was not.

Down below was nothing but rocky terrain. Nothing comfortable to sleep upon could be seen.

"I can feel how weak you are already, so be truthful to me child. Can you manage to fly for a little bit longer? There is no comfortable ground below us upon which to spend the night."

The girl shifted slightly before responding.

"I… I will try. I am very sore and tired, but I really do not want to make you late. So I think I can continue for a little while longer."

"Very well. I shall keep an eye out for somewhere to land and spend the night. But child, I want you to remember something."

"What is it?"

"You are not making me late. You are making us late. What I mean is that we are together, and we shall both arrive either on time or late. If we arrive late then there is no blame to be placed on either of us alone. The only blame shall be shared by both of us equally. I do not want you blaming yourself any further."

"Alright, I will try. Th-thank you."

The updraft had faded and Arisa now began flapping her wings once more to maintain their altitude.

"Now, if you are still sore you may unstrap yourself and walk around a bit to stretch your legs while I look for a place to spend the night."

"Very funny. I think I will be able to wait until we land."

* * * * *

The following day saw them near their destination. They had pushed themselves as far as they could in a mutual attempt to arrive before the assembly began but Elànde had eventually given up and asked that they stop for the night.

The morning of the fourth day, the day of the assembly, they had roused themselves before first light. Only the fading moon provided a small amount of light upon the forest.

Arisa supposed they only had maybe a

quarter day to travel. They would still be late but not as late as she had initially thought. Looking at the young girl next to her she was amazed at the child's ability to push herself to the limit.

Elànde for her own part was wishing she hadn't pushed herself so hard. Her legs ached something terrible, even after resting for the night. In fact they almost felt worse than when she had gone to sleep. It was difficult to stand. She didn't even want to think about how sore her bottom would be when she strapped herself in for the morning's flight.

Also, the provisions that Marika had packed for her were meant to last and keep her fed, not necessarily to taste good when eaten day after day. It had only been three days of travel and already she was beginning to wonder if she had made the right choice in coming.

"You are still tired. If you wish we can rest awhile longer."

As Elànde slowly shook her head she reminded Arisa of the small, stubborn child of ten. Arisa smiled to herself while watching the complicated expression on her friend's face. Despite having the stubbornness of a child, this was a growing fourteen year old girl who was giving it her all.

"No, I'll be okay. I just need a minute."

"After this is over you shall be able to rest for as long as you like."

"Thanks. That will be nice."

Looking up at the face of her friend Elànde smiled before beginning the climb onto her back. She ignored the protests of her arms and legs and forced herself into position and fastened up the straps that would keep her safe. Being so tired she was now very appreciative of all the effort that Marika had put into the harness. It might well save her life since she was not very likely to be able to stay upright on her own accord.

"I'm ready."

The exhaustion was easy to hear in her voice. Arisa worried for the girl but simply nodded and leapt into the air. It was still dark. The morning glow from the sun had not even yet begun to show in the east.

"We shall not have to fly long today. I believe we will arrive not long after the sun is fully risen. For now do your best to rest. I shall fly as gently as I can."

Elànde yawned heavily before responding. She was used to starting the days early in the morning. However, the flying had been leaving her too sore to rest comfortably. Not sleeping very soundly had been taking its toll on her.

"Thank you. I will be okay once I am fully awake."

* * * * *

"There is no reason for us to be involved in the affairs of humans."

Ever since the discussion began an hour ago, Nûket had firmly argued his belief that there was nothing for the dragons to do. He was a very young dragon and had very few interactions with humans. The much older dragon he now argued with was Maekar, the leader of this assembly. Sighing softly she addressed Nûket once again.

"Would you take such a cold attitude, Nûket, if it were dragons that had been vanishing without a trace?"

"The humans are good trading partners, and I do not intend my statements to simply be taken as a dismissal of what is happening to them, but it is not our affair. I would gladly lend assistance to any village in need if I were to come upon one being destroyed."

Nûket paused to look around at the other dragons,. He gauged their reactions to his last words before continuing.

"So far there is nothing to suggest it is anything other than bandits attacking the villages and setting fire to them. It's not our responsibility to hunt down every human who does wrong and see them brought to justice."

"I understand what you are saying, but the circumstances surrounding these villages are too strange. There has never been a single survivor. Not one witness to what has happened. And on top of that the distance between villages where this has happened is far too great to be a single band of humans causing trouble."

"Then what do you suggest, Maekar? That we dragons impose law on the humans? Do you intend that we spend all our time rounding up any human who brings harm to another human? That would make us little more than slaves to the humans themselves."

"You are twis—"

"For the past hour you have said nothing else. You seem convinced that this is something that dragons should be involved in. Yet I see no reason for us to enter into this. This is little more than a squabble among humans and until proof can be provided to show that it is otherwise I will not allow myself to become a patrolling dragon."

There had been quite a bit of murmuring from the other dragons during his last speech. Thinking this was due to his own statements Nûket looked around smugly at the dragons nearest him. They were, however, not paying much attention to him or what he had just said. Most of the dragons had their gazes fixed towards the west.

"Oh my."

Nûket whipped his head around at Maekar's soft words to see her also looking west. Quickly glancing westward as well he spotted what the rest were looking at. It was a lone, violet dragon in the sky flying towards them. A dragon with a human *riding* atop its back.

"My lady, if I may speak."

Another dragon had pushed forward from the crowd and was addressing Maekar with a playful expression.

"Go ahead Wuldaq, what is it?"

"I must beg your forgiveness for my dishonesty earlier, but I was not entirely truthful when I gave you news of Arisa arriving late. I thought it would be more interesting to wait until they arrived to share the truth of the human accompanying her."

Maekar snorted at his mischievousness. He was another fairly young dragon. One that enjoyed practical jokes. In fact he enjoyed them a little too much. She tolerated his playfulness, but even Wuldaq should know that this was not the time for such childish things.

"I shall speak to you in private later about withholding information from me, but for now speak the truth, and quickly. We can all see that there is more going on than what you originally told us."

Arisa was rapidly approaching and it would be no more than a minute or so until she landed.

"The human that arrives with Arisa is Elànde, daughter of Marlene. She is a survivor from one of the villages that was destroyed in this area many years ago. Arisa and I believe her village may have been one of the first to be razed. And I must beg your further forgiveness, but Arisa herself was somehow involved it seems."

At this revelation all the dragons began talking to each other at the same time, each asking the same questions the rest were asking. Maekar sighed and gave Wuldaq a look that sent chills through him. Shrinking back he knew that he had gone too far by keeping such important information to himself.

"Quiet! All of you be quiet!"

While Maekar tried to bring order to the cacophony of voices Wuldaq began pushing dragons out of the way. Deciding it was better to make himself useful than continue to suffer Maekar's gaze, he was making a place for Arisa to land amidst them.

* * * * *

Arisa had no doubt she was expected to land in the center of that chaotic crowd. It would not have been her first choice. For the past few years she had landed in nothing but wide open fields with plenty of room. Indeed, she did not even consider it polite to land so near others. In a wide open field one could glide in smoothly without causing much wind to those on the ground. Looking around she realized there was nothing else to be done than a vertical landing.

This type of landing always caused a lot of wind. Even more than taking off, which only took a few brief wing beats until she was high enough for the air turbulence to not bother those below. A vertical landing required a longer period of time to get oneself balanced and stationary before finally attempting to land.

"This is not how a respectable dragon meets others..."

Muttering to herself she began slowing her approach and called back over her shoulder to Elànde.

"Brace yourself. There will be much wind."

Back-winging, Arisa carefully centered herself over the opening being created as best she could. Thankfully there was very little natural wind for her to fight against. After a half dozen wing beats to stabilize herself she began easing off the strength she put into each beat of her wings.

Still nearly twenty feet in the air, the force of the wind from her wings caused some of those on the ground to look away. Arisa felt the strain in her wings as she was not accustomed to hovering in such a fashion.

Pushing her endurance to the limit she managed to descend another fifteen feet in altitude. With only a few feet to go Arisa slightly rotated her wings causing her center of balance to shift. Her rear legs dropped further and touched down on the ground. As soon as she felt she had a firm footing she gave one last beat of her wings to steady herself and then dropped, less gracefully than she had hoped, to all fours.

Turning to ask her companion if she was alright Arisa saw her wide eyed and gaping at all the dragons. It was similar to a look she had seen many times before on other children when they met a dragon for the first time.

Clearly astonished, Elànde had never imagined seeing so many dragons in her life, let alone in one place. There must have been nearly thirty dragons all standing in a circle around the two of them.

Arisa snorted lightly and spoke to the girl somewhat louder than necessary in order to get her attention.

"It seems you are just fine after our landing."

"Huh? What?"

Suddenly coming back to her senses Elànde was looking her friend in the eye now.

"Never mind. Come down so we can properly introduce ourselves."

Taking a cue from the new arrival's words, Maekar stepped forward and bowed slightly.

"Welcome. I am Maekar, daughter of Ishka. I have been chosen speaker for this gathering."

Arisa nodded her understanding but delayed her own introduction until Elànde had finished climbing down, though it would be more accurate to say she slithered her way down. Having had only a dozen or so attempts to practice dismounting she was still far from graceful. It was only after she was on the ground and had made her way to stand next to her companion's foreleg that Arisa began her own introduction.

"I am Arisa, daughter of Tirza. And this is…"

Elànde looked up at Arisa to see why she stopped talking. She startled slightly at the realization that her friend intended that she introduce herself. Looking around at all the faces of the dragons she looked pleadingly into her friends eyes. The eyes that returned her silent appeal were full of expectation rather than pity — and perhaps even a hint of humor.

"Umm. I am, I mean my name is Elànde, d-daughter of Marlene. Pleased to meet you."

Nodding to her companion, Arisa turned her attention back to Maekar.

"I apologize for our disruption. I believe Wuldaq shared the circumstances regarding our late arrival. My compan…"

"He did not."

Having been interrupted so unexpectedly, Arisa simply stood dumbfounded as she tried to understand the words just spoken by Maekar.

"What?"

The sunlight reflected off Maekar's scales as she turned her imposing frame towards Wuldaq.

"He did not share the circumstances. To be specific, he shared only enough to get a good laugh out of seeing our surprise and confusion at your arrival."

Cringing slightly, Wuldaq looked down upon the ground as he bowed his head rather sheepishly. Elànde found it to be a most impressive display for such a ferocious creature to manage and had to stifle a giggle from escaping her lips.

"Wuldaq had just begun to tell us the truth as you and your companion were coming into sight. He had started to say something about the two of you being involved in a village being destroyed years ago. I believe you should fill us in."

"Yes, of course. I will of course…"

Still recovering from her confusion Arisa was once again interrupted by a tapping on her knee. Looking down she was met by Elànde's tired face.

"Oh. Before I begin our tale, would it be possible to find a place for my friend to rest? She is not accustomed to travel and I am afraid I have pushed her too hard. If she may be allowed to rest while I recount what I can of our time I am sure she would be able to later share some of her memories as well."

Maekar shifted her gaze to the small child and considered the present situation. It was not forbidden to bring a human to such an assembly. However, she could not think of a time she had heard of such a thing happening in her lifetime. If this child truly was a survivor then she was more than welcome. After briefly considering the strange events of the past few minutes Maekar addressed the dragons around her.

"We shall take a short recess until the child is settled and Arisa is prepared to speak. Please allow the human to rest undisturbed. Wuldaq…"

Wuldaq winced at the hard intonation given to his name and the cold look he received.

"Wuldaq, you will stand watch over the child to ensure that she is both safe and allowed to rest quietly. This should not be a problem since you already seem to know more than we do about these circumstances."

* * * * *

"Aren't you scared to be here among so many dragons?"

Elànde was now settled in a small cave at the outskirts of the gathered dragons. It was far enough that she could not hear their murmuring, but close enough that she could still plainly see them look over at her from time to time. That is until Wuldaq had lain down at the mouth of the cave, blocking their inquisitive looks.

It had taken Elànde only a few minutes to retrieve her bedding from the harness. Even so, during that time she had become acutely aware of the stares from the other dragons. Though himself mischievous at heart, Wuldaq could sense her discomfort at being the center of attention and had used his body to block out the others for the time being.

"I am scared a little, but it is not of the dragons that I am scared. It is more a feeling that I will embarrass myself or Arisa by saying or doing the wrong thing."

Wuldaq simply hummed softly by way of responding and continued to watch the girl, obviously waiting for her to say something else.

"Is...is that so strange?"

The dragon lying only ten feet away from her flipped the tip of his tail a few times before responding.

"Strange may be too strong of a word.

Unusual might be more accurate. I spend most of my time traveling to different lands and villages. Most dragons fly for the purpose of reaching another village so that they can expand their knowledge. I fly simply for the joy of flying, with no real destination in mind. It is rare to meet a child that is not at least a little afraid when I show up."

The girl before him clearly tried to stifle a yawn causing him to chuckle lightly.

"Forgive me, I should be letting you rest and not prattling on."

"No, please go on. I am tired but would like to hear. Although… I'll ask you now to forgive me if I fall asleep while you are talking to me."

"Very well then. I promise that I won't take any offense if you were to fall asleep. You are here to rest so when you are ready simply close your eyes and ignore my ramblings."

Elànde smiled and thanked him while laying down so that she might still watch and listen to the dragon.

"Anyway, as I was saying, because I am so well travelled I have visited many villages. Most of them a number of times. And even at the most visited villages there is always a sense of caution and fear when I first land. It is not as if they really fear me, but I suppose they just don't know my true intentions. That and the knowledge that there is really nothing they could do if I were to suddenly go on a rampage…"

A wry smile crept onto his face before

continuing.

"Well, let us just say that I cannot blame them."

"Have you ever…?"

"Oh, certainly not. Though I suppose that could've been taken the wrong way. I sometimes have a short temper and have been know to fly off and release my anger in the forest. Let's just say what is left behind is best suited for scrap wood."

"I guess I can understand that. I have been known to break things when I lose my temper. You are so much bigger than I am that I suppose it is natural for you to break more stuff. That is what you meant by a 'rampage'?"

"Yes. And to the topic at hand, as I said I have never known a human to not be visibly ill-at-ease upon my arrival. Even if only briefly. But you are very different. When we first met at your village you were clearly nervous, but I had no sense that it was because you feared me. If I had to put into a word the feelings that I got from you, it would be to call you *shy*."

The girl considered this briefly. Was she shy? She had never really thought of it before. She rarely met new people. In fact she could count on both hands the number of new people she had met since her arrival in Rupsê. It would only be natural for her to be shy around somebody she had just met. Maybe she was a shy person? Just as she was about to ask Wuldaq what he thought about that he continued on his own.

"However, my expectations were entirely destroyed when you arrived here a short while ago. You showed no nervousness. If anything the only emotions radiating from your face were of complete awe and elation. I would not have been surprised if you had started clapping your hands and jumping up and down like a small child."

Elànde sat up straight and fixed a look of pure resentment upon her face. Her reaction caused the dragon to raise his head and laugh loudly. She did not think it was nearly as funny.

"I — I would never do something like that!"

"Oh my dear lady, do not take offense. It was a lovely sight to see a human, and a child at that, so full of excitement upon seeing so many huge dragons surrounding her."

Elànde felt her cheeks starting to warm and knew she was visibly showing her embarrassment. She lay back down and turned her back to the cause of her embarrassment. However, the dragon only smiled pleasantly at her and made no further attempt to rile her.

"Is it really so unusual for a human to not show fear towards dragons?"

Not hearing an immediate answer to her question, Elànde looked over her shoulder. The smile had faded from Wuldaq's face.

"Yes. I am afraid it is. I do not blame humans for fearing us. I have known many who have trusted me and looked forward to my return. But still, seeing the concern on their faces when I do return, even if it only lasts a moment, is something that is hard to ignore. As I said I cannot blame; I suppose I would feel the same way if I were suddenly confronted with a beast twenty times my size that could eat me whole in one gulp. That is why I am curious why you are so at-ease around so many dragons."

Halfway through this last discourse Elànde had turned back towards the dragon. Her only thought upon seeing his face was that he was truly sad.

"One of the few memories I have from before I met Arisa is of always wanting to meet a dragon. I remember asking my father many times when I would get to meet one. I can't say that meeting Arisa was a happy time in my life. It was truly the opposite. The moment I met Arisa the life I had known ended."

The dragon before her watched quietly, her sadness reflected in Wuldaq's large, yellow eyes.

"But, she never left me. To me she is family. I know I can trust her with my life. If she tells me to not be afraid then I know I can trust her."

"Then when you met Arisa, that is when your village…"

"Was destroyed. Yes. I don't remember much."

What could be described as almost a purring sound emanated from Wuldaq's throat. It was a strangely soothing sound despite how deeply the sound resonated inside the cave.

"You don't need to tell me. You will likely

need to recount these memories in front of the others and I imagine once will be enough for you."

Nodding her head, Elànde remained silent.

"I can understand why you are the way you are. Spending the last four years together, it is no wonder you have become accustomed to being around dragons. I wish more humans were like you, but that is our fault too. It is in our nature to not stay in one place for too long. I suppose I can't expect humans to change unless I am willing to change myself."

"I think I would have liked to have you around these last four years too."

"I'm happy to hear that. I also think I would have enjoyed visiting your village on my travels."

"Wuldaq?"

"Hmm?"

"Um, why do you speak that way?"

Wuldaq tilted his head and looked upon the girl with a confused expression on his face.

"What do you mean by *that way*?"

"You speak more like a human than like a dragon."

"Hmm. And how would you know how dragons speak? Have you met others besides Arisa?"

"No, I just thought…"

"That Arisa's speech was the way all dragons talked?"

Elànde nodded quietly.

"Do not tell her I said so, but the truth is that

she is the one who does not speak like other dragons. We dragons actually have our own language, though it is seldom used even when we are only among other dragons. It was long ago that we began to use the human speech for our own language. Most of us speak in the same manner as humans commonly do, since that is how we learned. A few dragons, like Arisa, feel that it if we are to speak a language it should be spoken properly."

The girl before him looked confused so he continued.

"In your language, you use the word *can't* instead of saying *can not*. Either one is understandable, yes?"

"I suppose."

"Well there are humans and dragons alike who believe that just because a word is understood doesn't mean it is the correct word to use. They say it is not proper to use the word *can't* because they believe it is not really a word. They claim it is an uneducated way to speak. I won't say that I necessarily disagree with them, but as long as others understand my words then I don't see a problem."

"Then other dragons aren't as concerned about proper etiquette and manners like Arisa is?"

"Well, I can't speak for all dragons, but I would say that the two of us are on opposite extremes in what we consider good manners. She is a very proper dragon. I am more, how should I put this..."

"Relaxed?"

Wuldaq gave the young girl a bright smile at the unexpected offering.

"Yes, I like that. I'm a more relaxed dragon."

The girl gave a small fit of giggles.

"Is that why you didn't tell, um, Maekar I think?"

"Yes, Maekar is the dragon who scolded me when you arrived."

"Then you didn't tell Maekar about me coming, because?"

"I enjoy a good laugh, even at the expense of others I will admit. Though sometimes, such as today, I can take things too far and cause trouble. I should have told her all I was supposed to but couldn't help but think of how humorous everybody's expressions would be at seeing the unexpected arrival of you and Arisa together. I suppose under the circumstances that was simply a poor joke, but it is certainly not the first time I have tried to have some fun and regretted it soon after. I am sure I will regret it even more this evening when Maekar discusses the matter with me directly."

Wuldaq gave a wry smile at his own expense this time. Shaking his head and looking at Elànde he could see her try to stifle a rather large yawn as she listened to him.

"Ah, I have kept you up enough. You should rest now. I'll make sure that you aren't bothered by anybody other than Arisa."

Lying back down the girl smiled softly and closed her eyes while murmuring a soft "thank you" before she became silent.

* * * * *

Maekar and the rest of the dragons had been listening, for the most part quietly, to Arisa's recounting of what happened to Elànde's original village. It had taken nearly three hours for Arisa to share all those events amidst the interruptions and questions. Near the end Elànde had awoken and joined them along with Wuldaq.

Now Elànde stood next to Arisa and waited for somebody to say something. Maekar was looking directly at her and seemed to be considering what she had heard.

"So neither of you have clear memory of what happened the night the village was destroyed?"

Both Arisa and Elànde shook their heads slowly.

"What of your memories from before?"

Arisa was the first to speak up in answer.

"By my calculations of the moon I have clear memories up until a week or so before. I do not know the specific point in time that my memory stopped, but I do have a gap in my memories. As far as I can recollect, one moment I was flying through the sky under the sun and wondering where I should spend the night later that evening. The next moment I remember is being awoken by this child, surrounded by a burning village."

Coming this far she paused and glanced at the child sitting nearby. What she wanted to say next she had never spoken of it to Elànde. The only person she had spoken of it to was Ketarr, and at that only very briefly.

"My missing memories, it feels wrong. I have had trouble remembering specific events before, but this feels different. It feels as if my memories were… erased somehow."

A surprised Maekar stared back at her.

"Erased?"

"Yes. Erased. I have a feeling that no matter how hard I think and focus my thoughts, I will never again remember what happened during those few weeks."

"Is such a thing possible? What potion could do such a thing?"

One of the younger dragons had spoken up the thought which was going through many of their minds. Maekar spoke up over the few dragons that had begun quietly talking to each other at the suggestion of a potion.

"While there are potions that have been known to cause humans to forget who they are entirely I have never heard of anything that worked for a specific period of time. However, it is something that was possible long ago without potions. There are stories that say the magicians were capable of such things."

Again the rest of the younger dragons began to murmur at this suggestion. Nûket stepped forward and spoke against such a possibility.

"But the magicians, the wizards were all wiped out long ago. And even then, the stories say none of their magic ever worked on us dragons. They were only able to ever make it work on their fellow humans."

For such a young dragon he was skilled at the use of words to make others agree with his position. Every time he had spoken today it was to argue against taking action or to provide some reason to doubt the story of the two.

Elànde watched as Maekar raised herself to her full height and spoke up once again to be heard above the growing clamor from the other dragons.

"We do not know why the stories say the magic had no affect on dragons. Much about that time has been kept secret, even amongst our own kin. Even if what the stories say is true there is no reason to think the wizards could not find a way to cast a spell on dragons."

Maekar paused and lowered her voice slightly before continuing.

"The wizards did not always exist. The last time they appeared they had taught themselves the secrets of magic. There is no reason to believe the same thing could not happen again. It has been three hundred years since they were defeated. If they could have risen once it is possible for them to have risen yet again with even more powerful magic."

Nûket clearly did not appreciate Maekar's point of view and merely harrumphed at her. The rest of the dragon's were clearly ill at ease, most of them looking at the human child in their midst. She was looking up at Maekar, clearly confused by what the dragons had just said about wizards and magic. After a moment, Maekar understood the apprehension of the dragons and cleared her throat before continuing.

"I believe that is enough for today. We will continue tomorrow at first light. Please do not disturb the human child needlessly. Over the next few days I am sure we will be able to hear more from her. Until then allow her some time to become accustomed to having so many dragons around her."

The human child in question had drawn very near to Arisa so that she could whisper a question to her.

"What is going on? It is not yet evening, why are they stopping so early? What was that talk about wizards and–"

"Hush, not now. We will speak of it later."

Elànde would have been upset by the short response but looking up into her friend's gray eyes she understood that it was not meant to be insulting. The girl nodded slightly and placed her hand upon Arisa's foreleg while she waited to be told what to do. It was a few minutes until the majority of the dragons had wandered off and left enough room for those that remained to move about freely.

"Come, let us go back to your cave. Then you can take this contraption off so I can give myself a good scratching."

The child suddenly realized that her friend had spent the entire day wearing the harness needlessly. Elànde herself had been sent straight to bed when they arrived and it did not occur to her until just now that Arisa might not feel comfortable wearing the saddle in front of all the other dragons. Wuldaq had been following the pair closely enough to have overheard their hushed exchange. He chose now to speak with a voice much louder than was really necessary at his distance.

"I don't know, Arisa. It is very becoming of you. It accentuates your wings very nicely."

Arisa gave Wuldaq an icy stare that would have been in strong competition with the one he received that morning from Maekar. Elànde looked back and forth between the two dragons a few times before noticing the wry grin on his face.She decided to play along a little bit.

"Ah, well, that is, Arisa. I'm not entirely sure I know how to remove it."

"What!?"

"I'm afraid I wasn't paying very close attention to Marika when she was describing how to remove the harness. We may just have to leave it on until we return."

"I.. I cannot believe you. How could you not–"

Arisa stopped mid-stutter as she noticed the smile starting to escape from the child's lips. The girl expected a sharp comment from her friend but was surprised to see her turn on the other dragon.

"You! You have been a very bad influence on her. I shall not allow her to be bullied into such things by you."

In response, Wuldaq did something that could only be described as dog like. He rolled his bulk onto his back and looked up at Arisa with the most amazing imitation of a submissive puppy that had just been kicked.

"What could I have possibly done to influence her? We have barely spent any time together at all."

Wuldaq lied so boldly and obviously that Arisa did not bother to remind him he had spent the past three hours in Elànde's company. Instead she simply gave him another icy stare that, unfortunately, dared him to continue his farce.

"A young dragon whelp is all I am with no ability to influence anyone at all."

Elànde watched, fascinated, through his whole performance and had managed to stifle her giggles until this point. Her undoing was Wuldaq actually wagging his tail back and forth to illustrate his point.

Arisa, on the other hand, chose to ignore his display entirely and turned her back on him.

"Come Elànde. Let us depart from his company."

As the girl ran after her departing friend she couldn't help but laugh as she looked back at Wuldaq, still laying on his back. He had allowed his tongue to hang out the side of his mouth as well.

Elànde caught up to Arisa and followed her back to the cave. Once they arrived she inquired of Arisa about Wuldaq.

"Are you very mad at him?"

"He is a child. I expect no more from him than to act like one."

Looking back, Arisa paused her speech briefly while watching the young dragon moving away on his own. The sun was reflecting brightly off his turquoise scales. It was not a common color for a dragon, though it did seem to suite him as he was not one for acting like a dragon himself it seemed.

"But, I must allow he stayed with you the entire time you were sleeping without once wandering off. However, you must not pick up any of his bad habits. And there are far too many for me to list. Now, if you please. Can we remove this contraption so I can finally stretch myself out without having it rub against my scales?"

* * * * *

It took more effort than Elànde expected to get the harness off. It was her first attempt as they had not wanted to waste time during their journey. There were only a few buckles to be undone, but even once those were free it took the two of them nearly twenty minutes to untangle Arisa.

It was a simple contraption but both conceded that they would have to find a better way to take it off and put it on in the future. There had been, after all, four grown adults helping to put it on the first time. It would likely take some practice to find the proper order of things when taking the harness off or putting it on.

Elànde now sat on her bed roll hungrily eating her dinner of dry cakes. They were not the most enjoyable but it was all she had available without making a fire and the only meal she had eaten that day. Her friend was sitting at the entrance to the cave, too big to fully fit inside, stretching and discreetly preening her scales that had been under the harness for so many days.

"Arisa?"

"Yes child?"

"Earlier when they were talking about wizards and magic, what were they talking about and why did they suddenly stop? Are you able to tell me? We have talked about it before so I don't see why Maekar shooed me away."

The dragon stopped her cleaning and looked, perhaps a little sadly, at the girl inside the cave.

"We have talked about the possibility that magic had been used at your village, but nothing more. Nothing about the history of this world. I cannot tell you all, but I suppose I can tell you some."

Before continuing Arisa arranged herself into a more comfortable position.

"There are some things I cannot tell you myself. I cannot say it is a rule or law, but there are some traditions that we dragons hold up as if they were law. To put it simply, there are some things that are not spoken of by dragons to humans. An elder would be allowed to share those things if they thought it was necessary, but for now I will share what I can."

The girl nodded slightly and leaned her back against the cool wall of the cave.

"Dragons and humans have lived in harmony for longer than history records on either side. It is true that a dragon would normally never live among humans, but our kin has always been on friendly terms with humans. We have provided assistance to them and they have provided assistance to us.

"In all that history there has only been one time when dragons had to fight against the humans in large numbers. It was a dark day in the history of both our races. A day when a group of humans finally learned the use of magic. It was the time of my mother's mother's mother when that day came upon the world.

"It is not precisely known how those humans came to learn the secrets of magic. They must have stumbled upon it by accident and so taught themselves. You heard Maekar mention this before and it is what most dragons believe. Even so, there are some that believe it may have been taught to them by dragons."

Elànde widened her eyes as she responded.

"But, does that mean that dragons can use magic?"

"No. I do not know the reasons but dragons are incapable of performing magic. In truth even saying this much is breaking one of our own laws. Dragons have always known that magic existed. Or perhaps it would be more accurate to say we know it is possible that it can exist. However, the truth is that we never found out how the humans came to acquire the skill for themselves.

"They were a small group at first so we dragons paid them no mind. That was our greatest mistake at the time. Before we knew it their followers had grown to an alarming size. It would not be wrong to call them an army. They kept their own secrets well. The dragons did not understand that they had learned more than just simple tricks until it was too late."

Arisa paused and looked down at her claws. It was clear that she wasn't done speaking so Elànde simply waited for her to continue.

"At first the magic users only used their magic to impress others. After that it was only to defend themselves from other humans. This went on for many years. Even when they became aggressive towards other humans, we dragons were still of one mind to ignore it. The magic they used was simple illusions and could not harm others directly. At the time, the dragons felt it was not their place to intervene in the affairs of humans. That was a mistake. We should have taken action earlier.

"It was not until these humans began to call themselves wizards and attacked and severely injured a dragon that it became apparent that the dragons would have to intervene. We knew then they had learned offensive magic as well. These wizards had begun to expand their territory, taking not just human villages, but also laying claim to the surrounding lands. Forests that had long been used by dragons for hunting suddenly became off limits. It was in one of these forests that the first confrontation happened and this was later considered the start of the war."

Elànde was now leaning forward and listening intently. She had never heard any of this before. Not from Arisa nor from her parents.

"After the first death of a dragon at the hands of a magician, the dragons of that land held a council. It was much like this one. They needed to come to a decision about how they should respond, a decision that all could agree to. It was decided that they would send three dragons as envoys to seek a peaceful solution.

"Only one returned to the council alive. After that messengers were sent in all directions to gather dragons from other lands. Even so, the dragons were not prepared for what they were up against. That war became the darkest time in our history."

Arisa sighed heavily before continuing.

"So many dragons were lost. Two of my great-grandsires and one of my great-grandames died during that awful time. There were at most six hundred humans calling themselves wizards. Even so, over four hundred dragons died before the humans were finally defeated."

"How… how could so few people have killed so many dragons?"

"The specifics are best left to an elder. But I shall say that the magic they learned had allowed them to become many times stronger and more powerful than any human should ever become. At the end of the war it was decided by the surviving dragons that the humans should never learn the truth that magic exists for fear that they would crave that power once again.

"Everyone agreed that it would be wrong of them to kill those with the knowledge of what truly happened. However, it was also decided that they would do everything possible to dismiss it as rumor. As dragons travelled from village to village they told fabricated stories of what happened. Over the three-hundred years since, the humans have forgotten the truth."

"Is that why they were all looking at me when Maekar started to mention the magicians? Are they afraid I will do something bad?"

"That may be a small part, but that is not the only reason. The other reasons are ones I cannot say, but rest assured they do not affect you. I am sorry I cannot say more than that just now."

Elànde shook her head and reached out towards the dragon before her.

"No, it's okay. I just can't believe humans would ever attack a dragon, let alone an army of dragons. I'm sorry to have made you remember all of this."

"Do not let it worry you, child. It was long before my time so I do not have memories of these horrible events. But it is true that it is painful to think of so many dying needlessly. In truth this has all been on my mind ever since I met you four years ago."

Elànde gave her a questioning look.

"As I said earlier, I have the feeling that somehow magic may have been involved in what happened to me four years ago. Even back then I had considered the possibility of magic, but like many here I dismissed the idea by telling myself it was impossible."

Arisa withdrew herself from the cave entrance and stretched her wings. The sun was now low in the sky and evening was approaching.

"At any rate, it is time I went to find some dinner for myself. You will be alright by yourself?"

"I will be okay. Would it be alright if I walked around a little bit?"

"Yes, just do not wander too far from this cave. And do not bother the others. You are but a small child to them, but even so they may be uncomfortable around you. These councils are rare and considered by some to be sacred times. Having a human here may unnerve them."

"I understand. I just want to stretch my legs a bit."

The dragon nodded quickly and then walked a number of paces away before leaping into the air and flying off towards the nearby forest.

Elànde stood at the entrance to her cave and watched her friend flying away. The evening was growing cooler and she enjoyed the breeze that drifted by. Thinking of those events four years ago when she first met Arisa had brought some painful memories of her own to the surface.

Looking down at the bracelet she still wore reminded her of how much she missed her parents. It had only been four years but already she had begun to forget how they looked and what their voices sounded like. Gently spinning the bracelet on her wrist in circles she whispered softly.

"I miss you. Mom. Dad."

CHAPTER 8

It had been three days. Three long boring days of sitting in the cave or walking around the edges of the plateau. After the end of the first day of the council Maekar had come to see both Arisa and Elànde and asked the child to not partake in the rest of the council unless called. Arisa had been upset at the suggestion but Maekar insisted that they needed to be free to speak of matters that could not be spoken of in the presence of a human.

Elànde herself had tried to soothe Arisa's anger. Arisa did not feel it was right to leave the child out of the proceedings but had finally agreed. That was three evenings ago, so it was now late into the afternoon of the fourth day of the council. They had called for Elànde only twice. Each time had been but a brief respite from the boredom as it did not take her long to share what she knew.

Although she was bored, she did not have to spend all of that time by herself. Arisa would come occasionally to check on her whenever the council would discuss matters that she thought unimportant to her. Even though Elànde had been concerned Arisa might get in trouble for leaving the deliberations her friend assured her it was fine. All the dragons would come and go depending on the current topic under discussion.

During these times Wuldaq was often with her, claiming that as a simple messenger dragon the specific details of the council were of little concern to him. In truth, she had discovered that he was nervous about his sister's wellbeing, when Elànde had finally asked him outright towards the end of the second day why he was so fidgety and kept looking to the western skies.

"Well, my sister was supposed to be back by the start of the council. I did not worry at first because even as dragons we sometimes run into trouble with weather, but she is now two days late…"

"I don't mean to seem rude, Wuldaq, but… I thought dragons didn't have strong familial bonds?"

The orange tip of his muzzle reflected the waning sunlight as he smiled.

"It is true, generally we do not hold familial bonds higher than any other friendship. The circumstances of my sister's hatching were somewhat extreme. In any event Naea and I became instantly close and I suppose I have always tried to protect her since."

Wuldaq turned to look at the girl and found her staring at him with a look of skepticism written clearly upon her face.

"What?"

"It's just… it's hard to believe you would be this concerned about anyone. You're so playful and, I hope you don't take offense, but you seem so carefree as well."

"Hah! Well I suppose I am, usually. I believe it's the same between you and Arisa, isn't it? I suspect you would do anything possible to protect her, even though she is more likely to be the one protecting you? In truth there is very little I could do to protect my sister that she could not do herself."

"Is that why you are worried, because there is nothing you can do if she were to be in trouble?"

"Yes, I suppose that is so."

"I'm sure she will be fine."

It had been two days since Elànde said those words, but there had still been no sign of his sister Naea. They had not talked about her since this exchange but Elànde could see he was still very worried about her.

* * * * *

That night Elànde was woken from her sleep by a great commotion outside the cave. At the mouth of the cave she could see Arisa sitting rigidly upright. Her gaze was fixed on the center of the plateau where a number of dragons had gathered. It seemed to be where all of the commotion was coming from.

"Arisa? What's going on?"

Without even a fraction of movement the dragon responded softly.

"Naea has returned from scouting to the west."

"Oh! That is wonderful. Wuldaq has been worried about h…"

The girl trailed off quietly. She could see that

her friend did not share in the excitement. Instead Arisa was focused on the gathering of the dragons. Looking closely at her friend she could see that the dragon was listening intently to what was being said, despite Elànde only being able to make out a murmur of noise from them. To her ears it was just a jumble of many voices talking at once.

Sitting down next to her friend Elànde waited for something to happen. After some time a loud roar was heard from within the gathered dragons. Every dragon not already gathered began making its way to the center of the plateau.

"Maekar has called to continue the council. From what I have heard from here I believe it best that you should come as well."

"But, it's the middle of the night."

"The news is not good, child."

As they entered the midst of the gathering dragons Elànde became anxious seeing the expressions on the faces around her. Some looked confused, she suspected these were the ones still sleeping when Maekar had made her call. Others looked troubled. No, it would be more accurate to say that they looked alarmed.

Once Elànde and Arisa had joined the other dragons in a wide circle around Maekar she could see that Wuldaq was in the middle speaking quietly with Maekar and another small blue dragon she couldn't identify.

If what Arisa had said was true, then this blue dragon must be Naea. Just as she was thinking this the two dragons left Maekar. The blue dragon moved to the far side of the circle and Wuldaq, to her surprise, came to stand beside her. He had been so worried about his sister. Elànde wondered why would he not go be with her.

Once all of the dragons were settled into place Maekar cleared her throat and spoke in a commanding voice to all those encircling her.

"This has been a difficult council to lead. In the end we have had to make guesses and assumptions, something by nature we do not take to easily. Due to the information just brought to us by Naea I feel it is important to end this council and invoke my power as chosen speaker."

Maekar looked around the circle of assembled dragons.

"Naea has been to a similar dragon council to the lands in the west and shared with me what has happened there. We now have proof that dragons are involved in what has befallen the villages. One cycle ago…"

Here Maekar paused suddenly and nodded towards Elànde.

"By your reckoning, that would be one month. One cycle ago one of their messengers came across a village that had been set ablaze. He arrived too late to do anything as all the villagers were already gone. But in the distance he could make out a number of dragons flying swiftly away. Being carried by many of the dragons together was what he described as a large cage. It seems the villagers were within. They appeared to be alive but were making no attempt at escape."

Unconsciously, Elànde reached over and placed her hand against her friend for support.

"The decision of that council is I believe the correct one to make and I am going to uphold their decision in our land as well. Every able dragon who is not feral is to immediately begin patrolling the air, looking for any sign of these renegade dragons. Naea was delayed in part due to the councils request that she stop at any villages along the way and warn them."

Maekar nodded towards the small blue dragon before continuing.

"For now, what has been told to the humans is that there are possibly feral dragons attacking villages and due to that we will be patrolling for them. The humans should be alert and cautious around any dragons that arrive in large numbers. While on patrol any village you come across that does not have two large trees placed in an X outside the village should be warned. After warning them place the trees as a mark."

After a short pause Maekar looked to Arisa and Elànde and continued.

"There is more that you should be aware of. One of the villages that Naea had stopped at to warn... it had already been destroyed. We have conferred with Wuldaq and based upon her description of the remains, we believe it to be the village where Wuldaq first met you. Naea found it like the others, burned to the ground and without any trace of survivors or victims. I am sorry child."

Elànde could not believe the words she had just heard and could only murmur softly.

"Our village? Ketarr... Marika..."

It was Arisa that was first able to speak clearly after a few moments.

"Wuldaq, you are sure it is the same village?"

"I'm afraid there is no doubt in my mind. I have never before visited a village with a large building built far away from the rest of the buildings."

"I wish I could give you both time to grieve over those you have lost. But we must take action immediately to try and prevent this from happening to other villages. We must travel the winds as soon as possible to warn all villages and spread the word to other dragons."

Lowering her head before continuing, Maekar addressed Elànde directly with a soft voice.

"Young one, I know this is difficult for you. I believe there is something special about you. You have survived two separate villages being destroyed. Along with the loss of Arisa's memories, it means there is more going on here than we even know. Now is the time to be strong for those that have been lost. I would ask you to have hope at the report that survivors had been taken captive from another village."

Raising her head she continued in a louder voice to ensure all the gathered dragons could hear.

"Because of the occurrence that happened four years ago to both Arisa and the human girl Elànde, as well as what has happened in these past few days, I have decided it is best for them to travel to the elders. That is, the elders of the dragons. If after hearing their story they wish to send the girl away and not involve her further then that will be their decision, though I do not believe they would dismiss her after hearing her story.

"Either way they can work with Arisa to try and recover her memories of what happened that night. Recovering Arisa's memories is currently our best chance at discovering what is happening. Until the truth is uncovered the best that we can do is to discourage any further attacks by making ourselves vigilant. The fact that this has been happening behind a veil of obscurity means they do not wish for a confrontation yet. We must buy time until the elders can uncover the truth and make a decision."

Returning her gaze to Arisa and Elànde, Maekar continued making known her decision.

"To that end, the best that we can do is provide them with the information that is available to us, which is in the form of the memories of Arisa, daughter of Tirza and Elànde, daughter of Marlene. Arisa, do I understand correctly that you have never been to the council of elders?"

Her hand still on Arisa, Elànde felt the reverberations of her friend's voice through her touch as she responded.

"That is correct, I have never journeyed that far north."

At this point Maekar paused once again and gave a heavy sigh.

"Though I do not intend to punish you with his antics any further, Wuldaq is the most well travelled of us all. He will accompany you as guide and protector and will treat this matter with all seriousness."

Without replying verbally, Wuldaq bowed his head deeply. Maekar then turned her attention back to the human girl.

"Elànde. This is a council of dragons that you stand among. We cannot force you or even give you orders. You are a human and may choose whatever path you wish. Arisa has already made it clear to me in a previous discussion that she has chosen to stay by your side and will not be parted from you. I apologize for the suddenness of this request and for these circumstances, but I believe time is of the essence. It is not a short journey, but please tell us, will you travel to see the council of the elders with Arisa?"

Looking around, Elànde saw every dragon was staring at her expectantly save two. The first was Wuldaq, who still had his head bowed. The second was Arisa. Looking up to her friend for encouragement Elànde found her looking straight forward. It was clear she did not want to force the child into a decision.

"I–I have nowhere to go except with Arisa. I will travel with her wherever she goes. I want... to find those that did this to my parents and my friends."

Maekar nodded once and turned to address Wuldaq, who raised his head.

"Wuldaq, I entrust you as guide *and* as protector to both Arisa and Elànde. Though you will guide them and have more knowledge of the lands, I am putting Arisa in charge of you. You will forego your usual foolish antics."

"I will ensure that they arrive safely."

Accepting his answer, Maekar turned her attention to all three of them.

"You should go and rest while you can. You have far to travel. The three of you will leave at first light. The rest of us must plan our routes in order to warn as many villages as quickly as possible."

Arisa nodded to Maekar and nudged her friend to move along towards the cave. They walked in silence until they reached the cave entrance and Arisa felt the need to ensure her friend was ready for the journey.

"Are you confident in your decision, child?"

"I'm sure. I have nowhere to go. You're all I have left. Everyone else has died. Everyone I get close to always dies, except for you. I don't want anyone else to die because of me."

Arisa looked to the girl beside her. She was about to refute Elànde's statement that it was her fault people had died. Upon seeing the girl's face she stopped short her answer. There were no tears in her eyes. Only sadness mixed with anger. Arisa could think of no words that would soothe the child just now.

EPILOGUE

Ketarr awoke in a strange place. Finding Marika asleep next to him gave a small amount of comfort. She was also beginning to stir. Sitting up he saw that there were people all around them. Most looked tired and dirty, many were coughing.

"Here is some water, it will help."

Turning to the voice behind him he saw a man and woman coming around to stand in front of them. The man offered a small bowl with water.

Ketarr helped his wife sit up and allowed her to drink first.

"Thank you. Where, are we?"

"None of us knows. My wife and I have been here the longest and we have not yet met any who know where this place is. Since we arrived many have come, though in the past few months it seems that new arrivals have shown up nearly every week."

The couple standing before them looked a number of years younger than he and his wife.

"Are there others from our village, are we the only ones to have been taken?"

"There are many others spread throughout this... prison. I'm sorry to say it seems that like all the others, the entire village was captured."

Marika handed the water to her husband and spoke to her husband quietly.

"At least Elànde left with Arisa."

The younger woman gasped softly before casting her eyes to the ground beneath them. The man put his hand on her shoulder and smiled softly.

"When we awoke here years ago, our young daughter was nowhere to be found. She also was named Elànde. They told us our village burned. She must have been left…"

The man looked his wife with sadness while Marika looked on with wide eyes. After a moment Marika managed to ask the question she believed she knew the answer to already.

"Excuse me, but — what are your names?"

"Ah, my apologies. I am Tobias, and this is my wife Marlene."

FROM THE AUTHOR

Whew. This took far longer to complete than I thought. Most of the story was actually written some time ago but some things happened that really delayed the process. But after having the story read through and revised a number of times it is finally finished.

I am amazed at how many times I read through the manuscript and would find small, but extremely obvious errors. I can't count the number of times I found the word "the" duplicated. I hope we finally found all the mistakes, but if you spot one please have mercy!

I'm thankful to my mother for her patience as she read, and re-read, the manuscript multiple times. Each time I got it back it was full of marks and scribbles which helped bring the story to life even more. It is incredible the change a single word can make and sometimes it just takes a different point of view to come up with that word.

I originally wanted to write a short story about a girl and dragon but I soon realized that the story I had in mind was really and after-story. As I fleshed out the *how* they came to be together and the *why* they were doing what they were doing I realized that I wanted to write the story of their meeting even more.

While I have no dreams of becoming a "real"

author someday, I just wanted to share this story. More for myself than anybody else. But if you happen to have enjoyed the story then it that would make me extremely happy. I do plan on continuing Elànde and Arisa's journey together. I found that I really enjoyed the creative process that went into writing this book. Besides, they have some new friends to meet and I want to give you a chance to meet them as well.

I wish I could say when the next volume will be ready but I just do not know. I am hopeful it will not take nearly as long as this one. Now that I have published one book I know what goes into it and can better keep myself moving forward rather than stagnate while waiting for things to happen (like proofs to be printed).

And thank you as well for taking the time to read this book. I hope you found the story interesting and I will strive to have volume two in your hands before long.

A certain day in October, 2015.

Daniel Hazelbaker